SAGA'S WAR

LEGENDS OF THE TRAVELERS
BOOK 3

by

Julie Campbell

SAGA'S WAR
LEGENDS OF THE TRAVELERS
BOOK 3

All Rights Reserved
Copyright © 2020 by Julie Campbell
Cover Design © 2020 by HarleyQuinn Zaler at HQ
Artwork

ISBN: 978-1-945893-20-9

Published by Untold Press LLC
114 NE Estia Lane
Port St Lucie, FL 34983

www.untoldpress.com

PRODUCED IN THE UNITED STATES OF AMERICA

10 9 8 7 6 5 4 3 2 1

Dedication

For The Morrigan

Author's Note

This series, and the connected Tales of the Travelers series, are books of my heart. Sometimes that makes them hard to write. I want them to be perfect. I agonize over details. Sometimes the solution evades me. So, funny story...because of the way this book had to end for various reasons you may or may not yet be familiar with, I had a really hard time figuring out how to write the ending. It took me the better part of a year of agony before I finally came up with the solution. Of course, when I shared it with a friend of mine, she was all... 'I thought that's what you had planned.' I about died. I guess if I'd had that conversation with her a year previous, you may have had this book in your hands a bit sooner. *hangs head in shame* Anyway, I thank you all for your patience.

I want to thank my creative team for their support. Jen, Sean, Shoshanah, Justinn, Debora, and everyone else who has helped me along the way.

Several of the horses in this trilogy are loosely based off of horses in real life, many of whom have crossed the rainbow bridge. I hope the humans who loved them enjoy seeing their horses in my work, and that I've done a small amount of justice to their legacy.

This may be the end of the trilogy, but it's not the end of the story. Happy Trails!

Chapter 1

Saga looked out over the grassy plains of her home world, before glancing back at her partner. Jarl stood on the edge of the forest in the shade of one of the big leafy trees. Brigid, another Vanier, stood next to him. It was probably the first time she'd seen them near each other and not arguing. Neither Jarl nor Saga had known that Brigid was a spy for the Travelers. Her partner, Dance, had been captured by the enemy. Jarl was nearly killed rescuing him and Brigid. Now he was here, with Saga and the others.

Flicking her ears in annoyance, she glanced at Dega standing next to her. Dega and her Alfar partner Aderyn were the unofficial leaders of this group of Travelers. It was Dega's fault that Brigid and Jarl had to stay behind while Saga and the others got the ingredients for the substance that would kill the Crystal growths. The other Traveler refused to let anyone tell the two Vanir where they were going, or to divulge the secret of destroying the Crystals.

The evil parasite controlled the Vanier and destroyed the worlds it grew on. It also powered the Vanier's magic. Dega was afraid Jarl and Brigid's loyalty to their home would prove greater than their loyalty to their partners. Dega was especially worried about the Crystal rings Jarl still wore, and what could happen if the Crystal itself found out they knew how to destroy it. If it could somehow control Jarl, that would be devastating. He was a very powerful mage, and not too many people would be able to stop him. Saga disagreed, believing Jarl strong enough to resist the Crystals, and knowing he was completely loyal to her. For now she went along with Dega's wishes, as did Dance.

Now Saga, Dega and a few others would Travel to Vanaheim to get the necessary ingredient. A fungus that grew on the southern continent near the crystal growths. Normally a harmless lichen, because it grew near the crystals it absorbed some of the magical properties and made it toxic to the parasitic life form.

Jarl wasn't convinced the Crystal was evil. Once she showed him how it had killed all the dragons, he'd believe. Saga knew he would. Saga had told him it was evil. Soon she would show him, and that would make all the difference in the worlds.

He'd been quiet the last few days, preoccupied. Saga had been so busy making preparations for the raid that she hadn't had time to find out what bothered him. They'd talk when she returned.

Ready? Dega asked everyone in the small raiding party.

Yes, Saga and the others replied.

Jarl waved when she glanced back at him. Brigid waved at Dance. Then it was time to go. She trotted forward when the others did, following them into the *Through*. Colors blurred and shifted from greens and browns, to blues and whites as they trotted out onto a deserted beach. The ocean surf crashed against a breaker reef offshore and the sun beat down on them.

They didn't linger, colors blurring again as they reentered the *Through*. Each world they bounced through made it harder for the Vanir to track them and made it safer for their home world.

Several more worlds separated the Travelers and their partners from Vanaheim. Specifically, the southern continent where the Crystal grew. It would take a lot of the lichen, mixed with other ingredients, to defeat the Crystal completely, but it was a start. Maybe, once Jarl was convinced, he could come up with a magical way of defeating the Crystals instead.

Finally, they came out of the *Through* onto a barren wasteland. The ground crumbled under her hooves, the air tasted parched and barren. The harsh sun baked the air.

Saga blinked and glanced around the washed-out landscape, looking for rocks containing the lichen. Bluish crystals glinted everywhere, pulsing slightly as if with a heartbeat. They thrust up through cracks in rock outcroppings and clustered in open spaces.

It would have been beautiful if Saga didn't know how insidious the Crystal was. Even now she could hear whispers in the back of her mind. Tuning them out, she took a few steps and inspected the rock pile nearest her.

Faiz said that the lichen grew in the shade. Dega came over next to Saga.

Obediently, Saga circled the rock until she found a spot that would rarely see sun and looked closely. *Here.*

Aderyn came over and knelt, inspecting the cleft in the rock. "I guess it's impossible to tell for sure, so we'll take everything we find. Leaving some for regrowth, of course." She pulled a knife out of a belt sheath and used the back to scrape the lichen into a bag.

Do you think the Crystal knows we're here? Saga glanced at Dega while Dega's partner, Aderyn, worked.

I don't know. Perhaps. We shouldn't linger, just in case. The bay mare tossed her black mane and perked her black-tipped ears. *I don't hear anything. Their mages surely know this world better than we.*

I hear nothing at all except the wind. No insects, no life other than us. Saga swished her tail in irritation.

The human in the party, William—one of the soldiers who fought with the travelers—had come on the back of Dance, since Brigid had to stay home. Rainer, though he said he wasn't ready to do so, had chosen another partner since Tomas had died. A female Alfar named Ima. Tomas's death was recent enough to bring tears to human and Alfar eyes anytime he was mentioned, but they were at war and Travelers were more effective with partners.

William crouched with Ima, scraping away at another rock. The Travelers assigned themselves hunting and guard duty.

Too keyed up to focus on hunting for the lichen, Saga paced around, tail lashing as she kept watch for trouble. The poor soil kicked up into a fine dust as she walked, covering her silvery coat and turning it tan in patches.

She stretched out her senses and even tried to listen to the oily whispers in the back of her mind. She couldn't quite make them out, and she thought that if they took notice of the lichen theft, they might change in pitch or urgency.

We should go, she said after a time.

"Yes, we have enough for now, and we don't want the enemy to sense our activities."

Saga, the only Traveler without a passenger, kept alert while the others mounted their partners. As soon as everyone was prepared, she led the way into the *Through*. The barren grays and tans melted into rich blues and greens as Saga, desperate for life to surround her, took them to a verdant world.

They paused on a white sand beach, listening while waves crashed against a reef. The air smelled pungent from the shoreline, salty from the ocean, and above all, alive. Birds sang and a sea creature called out beyond the reef.

She wanted to stay and bask in the vibrant life, but knew they'd hit several other worlds before they returned to the home world, and she was anxious to get back to see Jarl. Hopefully they'd have time to talk about what bothered him, and she still didn't know why he'd been wearing his formal robes when she had rescued him from his parents' attack.

∞ ∞ ∞

"What are you going to do now?" Brigid turned her attention from where their Travelers disappeared to Jarl.

Still not certain he was ready to believe Brigid was genuine, Jarl simply shrugged. Traveler partner or not, she'd been a thorn in his side for a while now, and it was her Traveler getting caught that had landed him in this situation. Clenching his jaw, he amended his last thought. Her Traveler getting caught had landed him in this situation sooner than he had expected. He would likely still be stuck having to choose.

Brigid still stared at him, as if expecting him to answer.

13

"I don't know." Apparently, the shrug hadn't been clear enough.

"You're the heir. Do you really think they'll let you slip away easily?" Brigid—who normally wore her hair up and only donned the finest clothing, had let her brunette hair hang loose to her shoulders and had changed into rugged riding clothing. He could hardly reconcile the snobbish court girl with the person who stood before him, a frown marring her pale face.

"I very much doubt they'll want me to be heir after this." He gestured toward the field where a few Travelers grazed. Then, hunching his shoulders, he folded his arms across his chest and sighed.

"Is that such a bad thing?"

"I might have been able to change things once I was ruler. Now, the only way to change things will be to fight." He didn't want to fight his family, his friends, his people. He was the traitor. Even though his parents had betrayed him and Saga, they hadn't betrayed what they thought was best for their world.

Brigid remained silent for a while, perhaps sensing that he didn't really want to talk about it.

"Do you think Ceridwen would join you here?" She finally broke the silence with the other topic he'd been avoiding thinking about.

Jarl had finally found someone who interested him and who liked him, they'd even been betrothed. He'd lost everything. Everything but Saga. He loved Saga and couldn't imagine life without her, however he hadn't understood how much he'd cared for his life on Vanaheim.

"No. She cares about her people and will want to stay and serve them." Or at least that's what she had implied when they'd spoken on this very topic something like a lifetime ago.

"Oh. That's too bad. I think she actually liked you." Her tone sounded neutral.

Jarl gritted his teeth and turned toward Brigid. "Don't you have someone else to bother?" He didn't really have to be nice to her anymore.

"I just thought you might want to talk to someone." Surprisingly, she didn't raise her voice. It sounded almost compassionate.

"Maybe I do, but certainly not you." He spun and stalked away from her.

"Thank you," she called. "I haven't had a chance to thank you for saving Dance and me."

Jarl hesitated. "You're welcome." He couldn't keep the anger out of his voice. He'd do it again, in a heartbeat, of course. He'd never let his people, or anyone, harm a Traveler while he could do something about it. That didn't mean he had to like it. Or her.

He continued back toward the forest where the small huts everyone lived in were located. He hadn't wanted it, but they'd given him Tomas's hut. He didn't need it anymore, and they were similar in size, so Tomas's clothing fit Jarl reasonably well. He'd arrived in his formal robes and couldn't very well wear them around the Travelers or their people without making everyone uncomfortable. Not to mention they weren't designed with forests in mind. The constant reminder of what these people had lost was rough, however. Tomas had been one of their own, and their only mage. One mage to fight a world full of highly trained magic users. Still, they'd fought, because they believed the Vanir, or more accurately, the Crystal that fueled the Vanir's magic, was evil.

Jarl twisted one of the rings he wore on his finger. How could a rock be evil? The Travelers and Alfar he'd spoken with swore it was a living entity. A parasite. All Jarl really knew was that it made it possible to cast magic more powerfully.

A couple of humans and one Alfar glanced at him and quickly looked away as he stalked past. Not in any sort of mood to be nice to anyone, he ignored them. He'd wait in his hut until Saga returned. There wasn't really much else for him to do except wander around and make people uncomfortable.

No one here except Saga and Orlinza trusted him, which was fair. He was, or had been anyway, the heir to everything they fought against. He wouldn't have trusted someone in his position either. That didn't mean he had to like it.

Following the narrow path through the old growth forest, he forced some of the tension from his shoulders as he got farther from the main concentration of activity. He just needed to be alone to think about what he was going to do, and to try not to dwell on what he'd left behind. He didn't think he'd mind being in exile so much if it wasn't for Ceridwen.

"Jarl?" Concern marred the normally clear tone of Orlinza's voice.

"Yes?" The one person, besides Saga, that Jarl would never be rude to if he could help it, was Orlinza.

"Are you okay?" She hurried down the path after him, and he stopped to wait.

"What makes you think I'm not?"

She smiled. "While people are generally uncomfortable with you because of who you are, they aren't normally running out of your path."

"Sorry." He stared at the ground.

"Jarl, it's okay. Do you want to talk? Brigid told me about Ceridwen."

Clenching his jaw, he forced down an angry retort. He would not treat Orlinza that way.

"No. Not really."

"I'll be here if you ever do. You should at least talk to Saga."

"I plan to, once she has a moment. She's busy with her plan to destroy the Crystal right now." Jarl kept his tone neutral. He still wasn't sure how he felt about it.

"She's doing it because she thinks it will fix everything. You know that, right? If there's no more Crystal, the Vanir won't be controlled by it, and your people can be free and you'll be able to go home. That's what she thinks anyway."

Jarl smiled grimly. "I know. But things are rarely that simple."

"I know that, Jarl, and Saga does too, but she wants to fix things for you."

"I wish she could." He wasn't sure how she could accomplish that, especially since he didn't know exactly what he wanted.

Chapter 2

Saga found him later. He'd given up sitting in the dark cabin. Even with the shutters open, the thick canopy blocked enough light that he'd have to use mage light to brighten the room. Instead he'd decided to do something useful, and so he'd gone around to the back to split wood. They always needed wood for fires and cooking and heat. Saga's home world was primitive compared to what he was used to. Of course, Jarl had no idea how to use an axe, so he used magic. It was quicker that way too, if not quite as physically gratifying. He'd amassed a large pile by the time Saga returned.

She trotted around the corner of his hut, silver coat shining, neck arched, and black tail flagged, obviously pleased with herself.

"Hi, Saga."

Hello. What are you doing? She sniffed the woodpile.

"Cutting wood. It seems to be a large chore without magic, so I thought I'd lend a hand. Do you think this is enough?"

Yes. I will tell Dega that you've taken care of that duty for a time. Others will come to collect it.

"How did your outing go?"

Good. We have what we need. The Alfar are working on it now and said it would be ready tomorrow. I will take you and prove the Crystal is evil.

Jarl knew he wouldn't dissuade her, so he nodded. "Okay."

I'm sorry I've been busy. Why were you wearing formal dress when I rescued you?

He hesitated. He knew he had to tell her, especially since so many others already knew. It certainly wasn't like he didn't want to; he simply didn't want to talk about it. To anyone. Even his best friend.

She lowered her head and the proud arch left her neck. Coming over to him, she nuzzled his shoulder. *What's wrong?*

He couldn't bring himself to talk out loud, as if that somehow made it more real. *My parents decided that I should be betrothed to Ceridwen. She agreed, so we were having the ceremony when they discovered Dance.*

How wonderful! She tossed her head, sending her mane flying. *Ceridwen is perfect for you.*

Staring at his friend, he raised an eyebrow.

She looked back for a moment before lowering her head. *Oh. Yes, I see. What will you do?*

"What can I do, Saga? I'm basically an outcast now. Even before we were betrothed, she had a bright future. I'm quite certain she won't get much backlash."

You could go back.

"I defended a Traveler. I fought back against my parents."

You didn't leave on your own. I carried you away.

"I don't think that matters." Jarl hung his head and scuffed his foot across the ground.

Saga nudged him again. *I'm sorry.*

Jarl shrugged "It's done."

Jarl, we haven't gone riding in a while. Get on. Let's race across the grasses.

To Jarl's mind, Saga sounded wistful. He understood how she felt. "Of course, Saga. I'd enjoy that."

Get on. Saga stepped over to his side. He grabbed her mane and jumped, swinging his leg over her back. Holding on to her mane for balance, he settled in while she wound through the trees and out to the wider paths.

They trotted past the evening fire. Jarl stayed focused on his partner. He still wasn't in the mood to talk to any of the others. If Saga spoke to any of the Travelers they passed, she gave no indication.

Once they broke out onto the grassy plain, Jarl felt Saga's muscles bunch. He squeezed his legs to let her know he was ready, and she leapt forward. Well used to his friend's speed, Jarl balanced easily on her back, body moving with her rhythm.

Wind blew through his hair. The last of the evening sun beat down on his back. Sweat from exertion beaded on his forehead, only to be dried by the air. Jarl shut his eyes, knowing Saga would take care of him. He let himself feel her every movement and adjusted his body to her. For a time they were one, flying across the plains together, air roaring in his ears.

Finally, Saga slowed, and Jarl opened his eyes. They'd reached one of the streams that bisected the grasslands around their settlement.

She stopped and dipped her nose into the clear water. Jarl slid off Saga's back and knelt by the water. He splashed it on his face before cupping his hands and drinking deeply.

If only life were always this simple. Run, drink, be with his friend. No worries beyond what they'd eat next and where they'd lay their heads.

Saga's ears twitched and she threw her head up. *I smell Skria.*

"Then we should go." Jarl stood and sighed. Even something as perfect as this, wasn't…

I think they've already passed, but you're right. We should head back. Shall we Travel?

"Whatever makes you happiest, my friend," Jarl said as he swung onto her back.

Being with you makes me happiest.

Jarl wound his hands in her mane and, inexplicably, blinked away a couple of tears.

∞ ∞ ∞

Are you ready to go free the dragons?

Jarl looked up from the bowl of porridge he'd been staring at. Not really hungry, but knowing he needed to eat, Jarl shoved the last few mouthfuls in. If nothing else, Traveling with Saga would make him extremely hungry.

"Almost, Saga."

I hope we're not too late to save Tala.

"Me, too." Jarl tried to muster enthusiasm about meeting a dragon. He simply couldn't. Right now, new adventures were the last thing he wanted. He didn't even know what he truly wanted. Putting on a smile for his friend's sake, he pushed himself to his feet.

"I will just put this back and join you."

Saga nickered and pushed his shoulder with her nose.

Not having to fake this smile, Jarl rubbed the star between her eyes, and headed into the hut he currently used. Trying not to look at the belongings that weren't his, and trying not to dwell on the dead man's clothing he wore, Jarl quickly cleaned the bowl and put it on a counter. He paused, leaning his hands on the rough wood and swallowed. Ceridwen's confident smile surfaced in his mind. He hunched his shoulders and wiped at his eyes before straightening and taking a deep breath. Today he would meet dragons, and Saga would finally show him why she thought the crystal that fueled his magic was evil.

Jarl?

Coming. Saga could sense his feelings to some degree. She had to know he was upset. So far she'd let him keep his feelings to himself. He was grateful, but he knew it wouldn't last. He just didn't know what to say.

He couldn't go back regardless, so it was not worth considering that option. He had, briefly, considered attempting to contact Ceridwen and seeing if she'd join him in exile, except that wouldn't be fair to her.

Putting everything out of his mind again, he left the hut. Today was a day for dragons.

Orlinza had already tacked Saga. Despite Jarl's insistence that she didn't need to help him, she continued, saying it made her happy.

Patting Saga on the shoulder, Jarl checked her saddle. *Is everything comfortable?*

Yes. Thank you. The others are waiting.

Jarl put his foot in the stirrup and mounted. *Let's go then.*

Saga tossed her head and trotted down the narrow path toward the clearing the Travelers used as a gathering point. Jarl ducked the one low branch and kept his knees tucked in tight to avoid banging them on trees.

Dega and Aderyn, along with Dance and Brigid waited for them. Both Aderyn and Brigid were mounted.

Jarl sighed but kept his opinion of Brigid's presence to himself.

Saga nickered and he caught a hint of sympathy in her mental tone when she spoke. *She's been a lot nicer since she arrived. You might give her a chance.*

Jarl grunted. She was right. As usual.

"Are you ready?" Aderyn studied him warily. They still didn't trust him.

Jarl was certain they tolerated his presence because of Saga, and because he was now their only mage. He'd have to do something about being their only mage. That, at least, he could fix.

"Yes."

Chapter 3

The Travelers all perked their ears before trotting out of the clearing. The colors blurred around Jarl, running like colorful magic. The world re-solidified around them. Sharp, cold air with a wintery bite prickled his skin. Jarl shivered.

Saga had warned him that they were going to the mountains, and he was dressed warmly, but the sudden change from warm, dry air to cool mountaintop was still shocking.

The Travelers stood for a moment and Jarl studied their surroundings. Vibrant blue sky with only a hint of clouds and bright, greenish-tinted sun over a mountain valley so deep most of the details were hazy. The air smelled fresh and sweet, and he took a deep breath. A few birds sang from the blueish trees. They all had needles and resembled the shorter pines from his home. These pines towered over him, even at this elevation.

The air felt thin, and he suspected he'd feel any exertion more than normal. They stood on a ledge overlooking the valley and after a moment the Travelers turned and trotted down a narrow path.

"What lives here?" Jarl studied the trail they followed.

"These days, wild game." Aderyn shrugged.

"They made this path?"

"Likely."

"Are there any humans or Alfar?" Jarl glanced around, as if he could find some sign.

"Not that the dragons said. They claim Dvergr used to mine the mountains, but I've never seen any evidence of that. Not that I've explored this world extensively."

"And now there are only dragons and wild game?"

"And now there are only wild animals," Aderyn corrected. "The dragons are dead, or nearly."

Jarl fell silent. He wasn't sure he wanted to know more and Aderyn was obviously upset. Brigid remained quiet while she looked around, eyes wide as she took in the sights.

The path narrowed and they followed Aderyn and Dega deeper into the tall trees. The thick canopy blotted out some of the strangely tinted light. Jarl patted Saga's neck.

Are you enjoying the adventures?

I would enjoy them more if my best friend wasn't sad. Saga twitched her ear in his direction.

I'm sorry, Saga. Don't let my mood drag you down. This is what you've always wanted.

It's what we've wanted.

True, and I still want it. I simply didn't expect Ceridwen.

We will figure something out.

Appreciating Saga's optimism, Jarl patted her shoulder. He couldn't share it though. His future with Ceridwen was over. He didn't like it, however no alternative presented itself. She would be okay without him. Ceridwen didn't need him to secure her future, but he certainly felt like he needed her right then. He would have enjoyed her council, along with Saga's. He felt the three of them would have made an unstoppable team.

The group rode for a time through the mountain trees. The Travelers' hooves crunched on the rocky path and birds sang in the distance. The air smelled so fresh, as if it had never been touched by another living being before Jarl. He knew that was fantasy, but he couldn't help the feeling of being totally alone.

They dropped down into a small valley and the trees thinned, giving way to grasses. The Travelers took a minute to graze and drink from the crystal-clear water before they climbed out the other side.

About three quarters of the way up the side of the mesa they aimed for, the ground changed from thin mountain dirt and rocks to powdery dust. The vegetation yellowed, as if unable to get enough nourishment from the parched ground and the stagnant air.

Though Jarl knew they weren't yet above tree line, the air felt as if it did little for him, and breathing grew harder.

The vegetation thinned and vanished, furthering the illusion that they were higher in altitude. The Travelers wound around the switch-backed trail until they crested the mesa. All paused at the edge of the flat landscape and stared. Mounds of crystals glittered in the sunlight, and the sight would have been stunning except for the dead quality to the ground and air.

After a moment's hesitation, Saga hurried forward, winding through the piles of crystals.

Tala?

Saga swiveled her ears around as if listening for an audible answer.

Jarl heard nothing, and from Saga's frantic ear swivels and wide eyes, she didn't either.

Over here, Saga, Dega said.

Saga trotted toward Dega while Jarl studied the mounds. He'd never seen a dragon, only pictures in history books. They were creatures of legend on Vanaheim, not something that actually had existed. He had an easier time believing in teleporting horses than he did in actual dragons, but he believed Saga.

The lumps of pulsing blue crystals were all regular shapes; oblong with one end taller than the other. He could almost imagine an impression wrapping around the outside that could have been a massive tail.

Dega and Saga stopped next to the farthest mound and both lowered their muzzles toward it and nickered. Dance with Brigid joined them.

Ahh, Saga, you've returned. Hello, Dega.

The feeble voice filled Jarl's mind, much like Saga's did when they spoke. Unlike hers, full of strength and power, the new voice sounded like a wisp of thought. Barely there.

Brigid put her hand to her mouth.

We can kill the crystal. We can save you! Saga tossed her head.

I'm afraid it's too late for me, Traveler. My body has failed. Only my spirit lingers on. Soon the Crystal will consume even that.

Not if we can stop it. Aderyn, please. Saga glanced over at the Alfar.

She dismounted and removed a pouch from her belt.

"I don't know how much it will take." Opening the pouch, she took a pinch of the contents. The light gray powder contrasted sharply with her dark skin. She held the substance for a moment before sprinkling it on a section of the dragon's crystal encased body.

For a moment nothing happened, and then Jarl thought he heard a shrill scream. Thin black lines

28

spidered out from where the powder touched the Crystal, and it crackled like fracturing ice. Blue liquid oozed out from the cracks and the light died.

Brigid gasped.

Jarl's eyes widened and he glanced down at the rings he wore on his fingers. Could the Crystal really be alive?

The fracturing continued, blue liquid pouring down the side of the mound until about half the Crystal had died.

Aderyn threw on another pinch of the substance, and the Crystal shattered and oozed.

Jarl almost expected another scream, or some sort of rancid smell. The only sound was the crackle.

You did find a way! Excitement colored the dragon's voice.

When the last of the light died from the mound that covered Tala, Brigid dismounted and hesitantly touched the remains with a stick she must have picked up from the trail.

The shards tinkled away, but it was obvious the Crystal had rooted deep into what was once Tala's body. They'd never be able to remove it completely.

Quickly, kill the rest before it cries out and summons Vanir.

Jarl frowned. "Can it do that?"

I don't know. I wouldn't put anything past that evil being.

Jarl lifted his hands and clenched them, staring at the rings he wore. Perhaps it was his imagination, but they seemed to pulse more rapidly.

Aderyn moved amongst the mounds, and Jarl found himself hoping they had enough of the powder to destroy it all. He still wasn't completely certain the Crystal was evil. It did appear to be parasitic.

It took some time for her to move amongst the mounds, but she did so as quickly as she could, not pausing to watch as the infestations cracked and died.

Brigid stood next to Jarl as they watched her work. "Did you have any idea?"

Jarl shook his head.

He stayed quiet until Aderyn returned to them.

"I got them all, but we're out of powder and will have to make more." She turned to Jarl. "Do you believe now?"

He shrugged. "They're obviously parasites, but evil? Controlling the Vanir? I'm not sure I buy that. Regardless, parasites should be controlled and not allowed to destroy someplace like this."

"Anyplace," Aderyn hissed.

Jarl didn't press.

She stared at the rings on his fingers. "It's controlling you, just as they control the rest of your people."

"The Crystals augment magical power. If I give up the rings, I won't be able to stand against most full mages at all."

"Are you going to stand against them?" Brigid looked surprised.

Jarl frowned and thought about what he'd said. "If they try to hurt me or Saga, I certainly will." He wasn't ready to commit to anything more than that.

She nodded.

Aderyn's angry expression didn't ease, and Jarl guessed his answer wasn't good enough for her.

Peace, my friends. The dragon's voice cut through their thoughts. *This should be a time to rejoice. You have destroyed the Crystal on this world.*

Is it dead? Saga sniffed one of the cracked growths, not touching it with her nose.

The only Crystal I can sense is on his rings. I'm well attuned to it by now. You have succeeded. Thank you.

Now what? Saga nudged the pile of rocks that had once been a dragon.

Tala sighed. *I will linger, see if the world recovers. Maybe someday the dragons will return.*

Saga's ears perked forward and she bobbed her head like a human.

Jarl got a sense from her that the dragon had a bit more than wistful thinking behind that thought, however Saga didn't share. It wasn't their primary concern anyway.

How long can you linger? Hope laced Saga's voice.

I do not know. Long, now that nothing, not even actual life, drains my energy. I would like to meet again, Story Teller.

Saga nickered.

"We should be off," Aderyn said.

Jarl could sense Saga's reluctance when she nodded.

He didn't want to leave the beautiful world either. Thoughts of staying, turning his back on everything and hiding away from it all distracted him from Tala's goodbyes. He couldn't though. He couldn't leave Saga, no matter what else he lost.

Saga nickered and twisted around to bump his leg with her muzzle.

Patting her neck, Jarl sighed. "I'm okay," he whispered. He would be, eventually.

Jarl, Tala said.

Jarl stiffened. *Yes?*

I know you don't want to believe, but the Crystal is evil. Or at least it is not benign. It has destroyed more

31

than my people. It has destroyed yours as well. I do hope we meet again.

Where did the Crystal come from? Jarl shifted his weight with Saga's movement as she turned to follow Dega and the others away from the fallen dragons.

If you find out, perhaps you can destroy it all. I don't know much, but I believe it is all tied to the original organism.

That would certainly change things for the Vanir.

It would change things for the Travelers as well. Your people wouldn't need to enslave them, with no reason to spread the Crystal there would be no reason why they couldn't partner with the Travelers instead for exploration. You would still have your magic; it would simply be different.

The idea intrigued Jarl. *Maybe,* he said. *Finding out where the Crystal originated from…that information must be lost to time.*

Perhaps. Perhaps not. Look to the Dvergr. I suspect they had a hand in its initial discovery.

They're merely legend.

I met them once. Some still exist, buried deep in their mountainous homes. Look to stories and legends for your answers. The Travelers and the Alfar are great bards. You will find the answers. Farewell.

Jarl started as the world shifted around him. He sent a hasty goodbye to Tala before refocusing on Saga.

The transition between worlds felt more abrupt this time. Perhaps because he hadn't been prepared. Dizzy, he clutched Saga's mane.

Are you all right? Saga swiveled her ears toward him.

Yes.

Find the Dvergr, and find the original Crystal…Would it be enough to prevent all-out war with his people?

He'd never be able to return home if he did something so drastic. He'd be a traitor for certain. But maybe…just maybe it would save them.

Chapter 4

Jarl watched as another Crystal growth crackled and died. The more Crystal they killed, the easier it was for Jarl to accept. Staring at his bare hands, he clenched them into fists. He'd taken off his hard-earned rings and put them in a pouch he'd then sealed with magic. He still didn't believe the Crystal was aware, but he didn't want to take any chances that it could somehow lead his people to him.

Blueish liquid soaked into the ground, tinged violet from the strange-colored sun. This world had two crescent moons hanging low in the sky, despite the high position of the sun.

Saga nickered when she came over to him. Her sliver coat seemed to glow purple on this world.

The growth that melted, cracked, and bled was a larger one. Aderyn had decided that they should target the larger growths first, as that would hurt the Crystal the most. Jarl agreed that it made sense. Tala's words still echoed in his mind. *Find the source.* So far he hadn't even started looking. Folk legends were all well and good, but the real information would be housed in libraries. Vanir libraries.

"Well, Vanir. What do you think?" Aderyn came over to stand next to him.

Saga and Dega scouted to make sure they didn't miss any of the growth. Brigid had, fortunately, joined another team. They went out in groups of four. Two Travelers and their partners. They'd destroy as much of the Crystal as they could, though the powder was still scarce. Jarl didn't know how they made it, but the main ingredient was apparently hard to come by.

"What do you mean, Alfar?" If she was going to call him by something other than his name, he'd do the same. He didn't want much, but a tiny amount of respect would be nice. He'd given up everything but Saga for them, after all.

Aderyn remained silent for a moment, before sighing. "I suppose I deserve that."

Jarl didn't reply. The violet-tinged light turned Aderyn's long white hair purple and made her almost black skin look even darker.

Dega and Saga trotted over before she could choose to elaborate.

We found one more spot. I believe we have just enough powder to destroy it, too. Then we can go home.

"Lead the way." Jarl followed his friend, weaving through powdery rocks the size of foals. The ground underfoot felt as rotten as any of the landscapes they'd come to over the last few weeks. If nothing else, that wasted, used-up quality to the land was enough to convince Jarl that the Crystal needed to be destroyed. The dragons had really been enough.

He saw trees in the distance, blueish, and reddish. He thought they were trees anyway. Sunlight glinted off what looked to be a large lake as well. The dead area around the growth extended almost as far as he could easily see.

Humans lived on this world. He suspected they avoided this area.

36

Aderyn threw some of the powder on the growth and the now familiar crackle of dying growth filled the too-still air.

Chill bumps ran up and down Jarl's arms. He frowned. Something familiar.... Magic!

"Aderyn, go!"

She didn't question him, simply leapt to Dega's back.

Saga galloped to Jarl's side and he scrambled onto her back.

"You're lucky I'm alone," a familiar voice said.

Conor! Saga spun around.

"Hello, Saga." He didn't sound happy to see them.

"Hi, Conor." Jarl studied the person who had once been his best friend other than Saga. He still kept his curly dark hair short, and his skin, several shades lighter than Aderyn's looked darker in the violet light.

"What are you doing here?" Conor crossed his arms. He wore sturdy traveling clothing. It had blue accents along the arm seams that would tell any Vanir he was a mage, if the rings that glittered on his fingers weren't enough.

"I had considered asking you the same question." Jarl met Conor's gaze.

Aderyn and Dega shifted around behind Jarl, as if he could protect them. Jarl wasn't actually sure he could. Conor was powerful, and the Crystal rings would augment his strength far beyond what Jarl could currently manage.

"I am looking for you. I'm not the only one, either. Fortunately, I found you instead of the others. Your *friends* are becoming increasingly obnoxious." He glared at Aderyn.

"How did you get here?" Jarl ignored the jibe.

"Your father dropped me off. He's due back shortly."

Saga, tell Dega to get out of here now. If my father returns leave immediately.

She says she will wait.

Gritting his teeth, he clenched his hands. They were all in grave danger.

"What do you want?" He appreciated Conor's warning, but he wasn't happy to see his friend. Maybe it was the reminder of what he'd lost. Maybe it was the way Conor didn't smile.

"You need to come home. Your mother…she's not well."

"She's never sick." Jarl's stomach clenched, fearing what Conor might actually mean. She wielded a large amount of magical power. Mages using less magic than her had gone insane in the past. If she were becoming unstable the results could be drastic.

"You should return. You'll be forgiven eventually. I won't even tell your parents that you're helping destroy our source of power." He didn't elaborate on Nessa's condition.

"I can't, Conor. You know that. Look what the growths do to the landscape. They're obviously parasites."

"A small price for the power they give us."

Jarl shook his head.

"Obviously they have you convinced. If nothing else, you should return home for Ceridwen. She misses you. We all do."

Wincing, Jarl squeezed Saga's sides with his legs. He couldn't quite bring himself to say it, but they needed to leave. He'd never be able to face his father, magically or emotionally.

"At least we know you are alive. Your mother thought she had killed you. What were you thinking?"

"I was thinking that I needed to protect Dance. It was nice to see you, Conor. Goodbye."

The words tore at his throat. He couldn't think of anything else to say.

"They won't stop hunting you, Jarl. You put your friends in danger by staying with them. Your only choice is to return home." He raised his hands.

Saga wheeled and they shifted into the *Through*. They didn't stop bouncing off worlds until they were certain his father wouldn't be able to follow their trace. By the time they finished, Jarl felt sick.

Would he really have used magic on you? Saga glanced at Jarl, before biting at her sweat covered shoulder.

Shoulders slumped and feeling as if he'd never straighten them again, Jarl shrugged. The monumental effort of raising and lowering them even a bit was almost more than he could handle.

They would pause on this world to rest and make certain they hadn't been followed.

"I don't know. If he thought it was best for me, maybe." Jarl longed to slide out of the saddle and sink to the ground, maybe even sink into the ground. The time it would take him to get back into the saddle could be the difference between capture and freedom.

"Some friends you have," Aderyn said, riding close.

"He did warn us."

"As if it wasn't obvious from his presence that someone with your Wayfarer ability had taken him there."

Jarl gritted his teeth and asked Saga to move farther into the woods.

She complied and Aderyn left him alone.

The sunlight appeared closer to what Jarl considered normal on this world, and he let that small detail comfort him and tried to ignore the silver bark on the towering trees. Lighter than Saga's coat, it shone almost like metal. The canopy above didn't block out the light like it would on his home world. He was tired and didn't look up.

I'm sorry. Saga nickered.

It's what I expected. Don't worry about it.

Maybe you should go back. She sounded hesitant.

No, I won't leave you, and I won't fight against you.

What do we do?

Keep trying to destroy the Crystals. It's the only thing we can do.

Saga tossed her head.

"Do you think they've followed us?" Aderyn rode over to them and looked at Jarl.

"No. Or they're being very clever." He suspected they were safe. For now.

"Then let us return to the Traveler's world. We all need rest."

Jarl didn't object when Saga shifted into the *Through* one more time. While he knew it wouldn't fix anything, he longed for the oblivion of sleep.

Chapter 5

Saga worried about Jarl. She understood why he wasn't happy. She had thought he'd at least grow content with their circumstances. Oh, he went through the motions. Currently, he and a few others were out in the field practicing magic. The first thing he'd taught anyone with a hint of magical talent was how to remove the collars off the Alfar. Now they practiced offensive and defensive magic.

She could also sense his dissatisfaction with having to teach them so rapidly. She knew it took years to truly master the magical arts. Some things could be learned quickly, and her people needed to be able to fight.

Moving to the edge of the forest, she looked out into the clearing just as Jarl hurled a ball of energy at one of the students. Tara, a dark-skinned woman from a sunbaked world Saga hadn't yet visited, threw up a shield. The energy splattered across it and Tara cheered. The handful of others congratulated her, and Jarl even managed to smile before he hurled another ball of energy at her.

This one caught her off guard, turning her dark hair bright green.

She shrieked.

Jarl and the others laughed, and Saga could imagine him admonishing her never to let her guard down. His light expression, though momentary, raised Saga's spirits. He'd be okay. Eventually.

Maybe there was something she could do to help, however.

Jarl, I'm leaving for a time.

Be careful, my friend.

Saga nickered, though she knew he couldn't actually hear her and trotted away from the forest, the world blurring around her as she shifted to a different world.

∞ ∞ ∞

Saga hid in the forest outside of Skeradder. The wooden wall seemed more imposing than last time she was here since she couldn't see what hid behind it. She wondered if they had a trap set up for Jarl, should he come to visit Ceridwen.

Maybe Ceridwen wouldn't even want to see Jarl, or her for that matter. Saga couldn't imagine what sort of upheaval they'd experienced since she'd taken Jarl away. It was almost too bad that his parents knew he was alive.

After watching for a time, she determined that, while the gates remained closed unless someone came or went instead of standing wide open, the other activities around the walls seemed normal. There might have been more guards than last time. She wasn't positive.

Ceridwen, she called out, not certain if she should or not. She had no proof that Ceridwen wouldn't immediately inform a mage of her presence, but she had to do something to help Jarl.

She received no reply, so she settled in to wait. Maybe Ceridwen was out. She often went on errands for her father in the afternoon, and the sun indicated that evening neared.

If an hour passed and nothing happened, she'd come back some other time. Perhaps after dark.

As the shadows lengthened, Saga pushed farther back into the forest and watched for any activity that might indicate she'd been spotted or that Ceridwen had heard her call, and betrayed her.

Nothing.

One last try. *Ceridwen, are you there?*

For a moment all remained silent in her mind, then, faintly, she heard a reply. *Come back well into the night, when humans sleep most deeply.*

Perking her ears, she waited, but Ceridwen said nothing else. It could be a trap, but why give her instructions when she could simply tell the mages that Saga was on this world.

She would leave, and then return. She trusted Ceridwen.

Leaves crackled behind her and Saga tossed her head up in alarm. It was only a ground squirrel. She took a deep breath. It was long past time that she departed this world. She took a step and the browns and greens of the forest swirled and ran like wet paint. Another step and everything went white, full of all the possible world combinations. She chose one and the colors swirled again around her until they solidified into an ocean-dominated world.

She stood on the beach, listening to the waves crash against a distant reef while she watched to make sure none followed. Saga had discovered that she particularly liked the grasses that grew just beyond the beach.

Satisfied that she was alone, Saga trotted across the green sands until she reached a patch of succulent grass. Nose down, Saga fell to her meal. She'd wait a few hours and then return to Ceridwen. Jarl would worry, but just as she'd known when he was truly in trouble, he'd know she was fine.

∞ ∞ ∞

Shortly before the appointed time, Saga returned to Vanaheim. She hid herself deeper in the woods and watched and listened. Nothing.

The night insects sang, an owl hooted, and all seemed serene. She settled in to wait, alert for any change to the rhythms of the forest.

When they came, they were far more subtle than Saga had expected.

The owl continued to hoot, though it did change trees. That small shift alerted Saga to some other presence in the forest. She didn't hear anyone move.

Tense, ready to leave the world if necessary, she listened with perked ears and quivering muscles.

Saga? Ceridwen's hesitant voice broke the silence.

I'm here.

We're coming. You'll have to tell me where to find you. I can't follow your mental voice like Jarl can.

We?

I've brought Alfar. You must rescue them. Nessa has decided they're the cause for Jarl's abduction. She's having them murdered. I can't do much. I've saved a few.

It's not a trap for Jarl?

That may be her true motivation. If it is, I have not been told.

Saga thought for a moment. Ceridwen could be lying, but she'd always been honest in the past and Saga could sense that she cared for Jarl. The emotion

44

came through the conversation when she thought about him. Saga would have to trust that.

I'm over here. She snapped a twig.

We're coming.

How many?

Three Alfar, and myself.

Okay. Saga listened. The Alfar moved quietly, as did Ceridwen, but shortly she made out the individual sounds of their breathing. Flaring her nostrils, she took in the scents and thought she smelled four distinct body odors, too. Ceridwen she recognized. The other three smelled unwashed.

"Saga," Ceridwen said in hushed tones when she came close. "You're very good at hiding in the dark."

Yes.

"Can you take these three Alfar?"

Yes. How did you rescue them?

"Lady Alis is sympathetic to their cause as well. We engineered their 'escape.'"

I came to ask you how you were.

"I am doing all right. I miss you and Jarl, but I don't let anyone know. I believe that is for the best, as Conor told Nessa that Jarl is alive and willing to stay away from Vanaheim. She's very upset. I'm trying to stay in their good graces. I might be able to help."

Jarl misses you as well. You wouldn't consider leaving?

"I wish I could, Saga. My people need me." She hung her head for a moment.

Saga sensed regret in her voice.

"I do not believe I will be able to rescue more Alfar. Nessa is becoming insistent that they all be killed. Only people's reliance upon them has kept many alive thus far. These three came from Mageheim. All the Alfar have been ejected from the school and surrounding village. Many came through here, since we are close."

I will tell the others they must be rescued. Without knowing their locations, I'm not sure we will be able to do much. We will do what we can.

"Thank you. The more I consider Nessa's state of mind, the more I suspect a trap. Be careful."

Thank you. Please consider joining us.

Ceridwen nodded even though Saga knew she wouldn't.

She turned her attention fully to the Alfar. They looked half starved, even worse than most Alfar were kept. Scabs ringed their wrists and one, the male with skin as pale as Orlinza's, had a swollen eye.

You will all have to mount.

They glanced at Ceridwen before nodding.

Saga found a nearby fallen tree and went and stood next to it. Ceridwen helped them onto Saga's back.

Even emaciated, three Alfar were heavy. Saga wouldn't go far. She'd take them to a reasonably safe world, then bring help. It didn't seem wise to bring anything directly to her home world from Vanaheim.

Maybe the world with the pies. She could use a pie, and so could the Alfar. Yes. She'd go there.

"Be careful, Saga." Ceridwen rubbed her muzzle.

You as well. Thank you for letting me know about the Alfar. What had you planned to do with them, if I hadn't come?

She studied the ground. "Keep them hidden as long as I could. I had hoped you or Jarl would come one last time. I didn't have a better plan than that."

The Alfar remained silent.

I must go. I'm sure the others are worried. I want to see you again, Ceridwen.

46

"I want to see both of you again under better circumstances. Please tell Jarl I'm all right, and that I do miss him, but not to let that worry him."

I will. Once we destroy the Crystal, maybe we can return.

"Destroy it?" Ceridwen glanced to the Alfar, who all had a small chip of Crystal pulsing at their necks. "Why?"

Saga sighed. She'd forgotten that Ceridwen didn't know. *It is evil. It controls the Vanir and it destroys the land around it.*

Ceridwen frowned. "Truly?"

Nodding, Saga swished her tail in agitation. She shouldn't have said anything.

"And no one knows this?"

The Alfar knew, once. That is the origin of the war. They tried to destroy it. The humans fought back, already infected by its power.

Her eyebrows rose. "I see. I will keep this knowledge to myself, as there is only one place I could have learned it. I do not wish to be under suspicion."

Yes, do so. No one would believe you anyway. Be well, Ceridwen. Until we meet again. Saga bumped Ceridwen's shoulder with her nose and turned away.

She shifted worlds as quickly as she could, touching several before settling on the world with the pie. It was early morning when they arrived in a meadow. The air smelled fresh, and moisture hung heavy in a low mist along the ground. Dew glistened on bright green foliage where the fog had burnt away. A few late flowers bloomed among the grasses and a stand of trees bordered on edge.

She saw several horses grazing near the wood and headed that direction.

I will leave you here for now. I must bring help, for I cannot carry three the entire way. First, I will bring you something to eat.

"Thank you," one of the women said.

Once they reached the wood, the three Alfar slid from her back. They looked around nervously, and the man reached to the collar at his throat before dropping his hand, as if burned. They didn't question her

Stay here. I will return.

They all sank to the ground, backs to trees.

Satisfied that they were reasonably well hidden amongst the old oaks, she tossed her mane and headed toward the small town at a trot, looking forward to a treat and hoping she could figure out a way carry several back for the Alfar.

Chapter 6

Jarl glanced out into the field again, wondering where Saga had gone. It wasn't the first time she'd disappeared for a longer period. Usually he knew where she had gone, or at least what her mission was.

Why did he even bother to look? He'd know when she returned; he'd sense her presence. Then she'd tell him what she'd been doing.

Gritting his teeth, Jarl headed for his hut. Those he trained in magic seemed to like him well enough. Everyone else either gave him mistrustful looks anytime he came by, or actively avoided him unless they had no choice. He pushed his students hard because he didn't have much time to train them, and he wanted to keep them safe. Ironically, the Alfar seemed most comfortable in his presence. Perhaps because he'd been the one to remove their collars.

It wouldn't be long before he'd have to start searching for the source of the Crystal, and the chances of him getting captured were high. He needed access to the Vanir libraries. He also needed to tell Saga his plan, but hesitated. She would want to help, but she couldn't go back to Vanaheim. He didn't want to lose her, too.

Looking for something to do to kill time, Jarl thought about splitting more wood. Apparently, he'd already cut enough for their village to last a year or more. They'd started sending the wood to other settlements.

Maybe there was something else useful he could be doing besides teaching mages. As he cast about for something to do, he felt Saga's presence strengthen. She'd returned.

Abandoning his search for a useful task, Jarl picked his way through the woods until he reached the path that led to the meadow. His shoulders brushed against the occasional trunk as he wound through the trees. Old rotted leaves gave way to grasses and the late evening sun shone in his eyes as he reached the clearing. Blinking in the harsh light, he headed toward his friend.

Dega and a few other Travelers already crowded around Saga. Though they could speak over distances, they were very horse-like in many ways and enjoyed proximity.

Aderyn and Brigid jogged out of the trees and headed for the group of Travelers. Something had happened.

Picking up his pace, Jarl trotted over to the others.

Jarl. Saga touched his arm with her nose.

He patted her neck. *What's wrong?*

Nessa is killing the Alfar. We must rescue them.

Bumps raced up his arms and he shivered.

I brought three with me. I didn't want to bring them directly here.

Jarl blinked. *Wait a moment. Did you go to Vanaheim?*

Saga bobbed her head.

It's not safe. You shouldn't have gone. How did you rescue the Alfar? How do you know my mother is killing them?

50

She snorted. *I went to talk to Ceridwen. She told me. She also asked me to tell you that she misses you, but not to let that worry you. She's doing fine.*

Jarl snapped his mouth shut on a retort. Ceridwen missed him? The pain that had scabbed over ripped open again. He clenched his hands into fists.

I'm sorry. Should I not have told you?

No, I'm glad you did. Thank you. I miss her, too. Where are the Alfar you rescued? He could get the full story later.

I wasn't sure if it was safe to bring them directly here now that the Vanir know we're rescuing them. I left them someplace safe. We need to go make sure they're not being tracked.

Jarl nodded. "Okay, Saga. Let's go get the Alfar. We need a few Travelers to come with us." He glanced around and a couple of the others bobbed their heads, ears perked forward.

"I will go as well," Aderyn said.

"Saga, would you ask Rainer to have Ima join us? I want her to come along as well. She's doing well with her magic and she could use the practice removing the collars."

Yes.

It didn't take long before the light gray Traveler cantered up with Ima, a fair skinned Alfar perched on his back. She wore her white hair short, and vibrant sea green eyes studied Jarl.

She was currently his most promising student.

"Yes, Jarl?"

"I'd like you to join us. We're going to collect some Alfar and remove their collars."

She nodded sharply and Rainer turned and touched noses with Saga and Dega. Aderyn and Jarl mounted, and after a quick discussion, they decided that each of the three Travelers could take an Alfar along with their partner. That way if they were too weak to ride on their own, they'd have some support.

Saga took the lead, and they headed out across the grasslands.

The colors swirled and melted around Jarl as she took them into the *Through*. Saga had become adept at touching other worlds to mar their trace without actually having to completely appear on that world. She bounced off several before a scene similar to the grasslands he'd just left shimmered into view around him. Long, bright green grasses swayed in a gentle breeze. A stand of tall, white-bark trees concealed the horizon from view. When Jarl glanced around himself, he saw more of the grasses. It looked more like a cultivated pasture than true wild grasslands, the grass more uniform in type. In the distance he saw clumps of horses grazing.

"Where are we?" He glanced up at the sky. The sun was low in the horizon, and it seemed to be late afternoon, but he wasn't positive. It could have been early in the day. He'd seen worlds where the sun tracked backward across the sky from what he was used to.

The world with the pie. I will show you sometime.

That explanation seemed to make perfect sense to Saga, but left Jarl perplexed. It didn't matter, so he put it out of his mind. He did notice that Rainer and Dega both perked up when Saga mentioned pie.

They're over here.

The Travelers headed to the stand of trees and stopped just outside. Jarl could just make out the outline of three huddled figures amongst the trees. One stood after a moment and slowly approached. His eyes tracked over the riders, and his shoulders eased when his gaze landed on Saga. He did frown when he saw Jarl.

Jarl sighed, ignoring it. He didn't think he was recognizable as Vanir without any of his rings, or normal clothing. Apparently, they could tell.

These Alfar are from Mageheim. It's possible they've seen you before.

Ahh. He patted Saga's shoulder. "Ima, would you care to remove their collars."

She shot a quick, almost nervous glance at Jarl before swallowing and nodding her head in a sharp jerk. Dismounting, she approached the other Alfar.

"I'm going to take those off of you."

He put his hand up to his throat before dropping it and nodding. "Thank you."

Jarl winced at the scabs around his wrists and the sunken look to his cheeks. Most Alfar were thin, but he was emaciated.

Ima put her hands to the collar and shut her eyes in concentration.

Magical energies gathered around them as she muttered words she'd developed to help her focus on the task. It wasn't easy to remove the collars, at least not for someone with very little magical practice, but it wasn't the most difficult task she'd ever done at Jarl's direction. She'd never had a chance to practice the spell in actuality, though she'd performed the magic a few times.

For a moment, Jarl thought she might fail, then the collar fell away from the Alfar's neck. Ima's eyes snapped open and she smiled, eyes bright.

She glanced at Jarl.

He gave her the warmest smile he could currently manage and nodded. "Well done. Why don't you see to the other two as well?"

53

Buoyed by her success, she hurried toward the other two.

Rainer went with her, unwilling to let his new partner out of his sight on a potentially dangerous world. Not after having so recently lost Tomas.

Aderyn dismounted and went over to the Alfar. "What's your name?"

He shook his head. "The Vanir called me Orsi, but I wish a new name. I will think on it."

Aderyn nodded. "Let us know when you decide. Do you need anything, are you or your companions seriously injured?"

"No. Our injuries are minor. They are killing our people on Vanaheim. We would be dead if not for Lady Ceridwen and Lady Ailis." He glanced at Jarl. "You will help the others?"

Not quite sure why the Alfar picked him specifically, Jarl hesitated, then nodded. What else could he do? "We will do our best... I will do my best."

Have you overheard anything, or do you know anything that will help us? Saga perked her ears forward.

"I will tell you everything I can. Though I don't know what one such as I can do to help."

Saga stomped the ground with her foot. *You can do plenty.*

He took a step back at the force of Saga's displeasure before dropping his gaze.

"I'm sorry."

She snorted. *None of that. You are free. Do not apologize. Come, Ima has finished. Let us return home so we can plan our rescues.*

Seemingly on the verge of apologizing again, he instead nodded and came over to her side when Jarl held out his hand.

"You can ride behind me."

"Thank you."

Jarl kicked his foot out of the stirrup and helped the Alfar mount. Ima returned holding three collars as if they might bite her. The two other Alfar, both women in as bad a shape as their companion followed, blinking in the sunlight as if they'd lived in shade their whole lives.

Sickened, Jarl turned his gaze away and began to make plans. He had to find the source of the Crystal, but clearly the Alfar needed to be rescued first. They were in grave danger.

Chapter 7

"You do know this is a trap, don't you?" Brigid crossed her arms and glared at Jarl.

"What else can we do? We have to rescue as many of them as we can. They haven't done anything wrong."

Saga paused her grazing to nicker.

"That's not what our people believe. They believe the Alfar started the war."

Jarl glared back. Brigid was infuriating, even when she wasn't being blatantly unpleasant as she had before he'd saved her Traveler. "What do you believe?" He wished the question would redirect the conversation. He leaned against a tree, the rough bark digging into his shoulder through the thin fabric of his shirt.

"I would guess that the truth is somewhere in the middle, as histories are usually written by the victor, and our people did win that war." She twisted her hands in front of her and turned away, looking out over the grasslands of the Travelers' home world.

Why would that admission make Brigid uncomfortable? Jarl just shrugged. He had no idea what Brigid thought most of the time. "I'm not sure it really matters now. The war was long ago and the Alfar have learned their lesson. It's time to move on."

"Learned their lesson?" Aderyn growled, coming up beside Jarl.

"Yes, that the Vanir cannot be trusted with power. When next they strike, in this case, soon, they, and we, shall have to be more careful. Perhaps if we could convince the others to release the Alfar and stop trying to enslave other races, we could all move on in a different direction. That won't happen, at least not while the Crystal exists, and we will have to proceed with war."

Saga, standing off a short distance grazing with Dance, tossed her head in approval.

"So, we rescue the Alfar. You know you can't go back. We have to send others." Brigid unfolded her arms and sank to the loamy ground.

Aderyn joined her, leaving Jarl standing by the tree. He just wished he didn't feel so alone.

"Of course, I have to go. I'm the only one with any chance of fighting back against mages."

"Ima—"

"Is not trained enough to combat full mages. She and the others have potential. They're simply not ready."

"If you get captured," Aderyn interjected, "they will never be ready."

"I've taught them what I can for now. They need practice." Jarl clenched his jaw and walked away from the women.

"You know we're right, Jarl," Aderyn called after him.

"I get the impression most of you would rather have me gone." He walked away before the others could reply.

Jarl?

It's nothing, Saga. I just want to be alone for a while.

You are always alone.

58

I know.

He felt Saga's annoyance, but she left him alone. He walked deeper into the woods, not wanting to bother anyone with his foul mood.

"Jarl?"

He hadn't gotten terribly far before Orlinza caught up to him.

"Yes?"

"Saga told me I should probably leave you alone, but I need some information from you to plan our rescue attempts. Do you mind?" She came up next to him, all hints of diffidence gone from her bearing.

Her transformation over such a short time amazed him. Most of the other recently freed Alfar were still hesitant and uncertain of themselves. Orlinza had taken to freedom immediately, or so it had seemed. Perhaps years in Saga's employ, as it were, had made it easier for her to accept her new life.

"Of course, Orlinza. Anything you need." Suppressing his ill mood as much as he could, Jarl turned and followed her back toward the common area of the camp. Though outside, that was where most of the planning was accomplished. The differences in the small camp simply drove home all the differences between his former life and now. The only thing he truly missed, besides Ceridwen, was easy access to warm baths.

Smiling at that thought, he joined the others around the fire circle.

∞ ∞ ∞

Scouts had returned with word on several holding locations. Jarl had finally convinced the others to let him go along on the mission, if only because he could take a larger group of the Alfar than an individual Traveler could. Their plan was to stage Travelers on the world Saga claimed had delicious pie. He and a few others would sneak in, get the Alfar and return indirectly to that world. From there the Travelers would scatter to confuse the trace even further, then everyone would meet on the home world, if all went well.

So much could go wrong, but they had to try. Everyone agreed on that point.

They'd take just one Traveler with them, fitted out with traditional Vanir tack. By the expression on Dega's face, she was disgusted by the bar of metal in her mouth.

Saga's coloring was too distinctive for her to go, and Aderyn had to stay behind as well. Dega's dark bay coloring was common on the Vanir home world. Jarl cast a small glamour to hide the white markings across her withers. She'd fit right in. Jarl also cast a minor glamour over himself, lengthening his wavy hair, darkening his eyes and skin slightly, and adjusting his height by an inch. It would have to do. Drastic changes were hard for the person wearing the glamour to accommodate in their movements, giving them away to anyone observant or on the lookout for magical disguises. With a relatively stable reign for the past many years, magical disguises weren't common. Guards were still trained to watch for such things. Just in case.

William and Ari gathered close.

Ari should ride, Dega said to the group. He wore the finest clothing amongst them.

William glanced at Jarl and then up at Ari. "We off then?" He sounded nervous, though he was a seasoned fighter.

Jarl hoped it was simply straight nerves and not something else. "Yes."

Glancing at Jarl again, William clenched his jaw and jerked his head.

Maybe he was nervous about Jarl.

Be careful. I will see you soon, Saga said.

You as well, my friend. Jarl turned his attention to his task. They would go to one other world before returning to Vanaheim. It was much more difficult to track where someone had come from, then to track where someone was going, and Jarl wasn't too worried about that. By the time anyone knew he was on the world, he'd be gone.

Gathering his magic around him, he fixed the location of the first world the Travelers had taken him to in his mind. The dry, cracked dirt, the towering Crystal spire, the broken dusty air and the sense he had of the world that any Farer would develop once they'd visited a place. He combined those feels and reached as they walked forward.

The effort of transporting even a small group over such a distance staggered Jarl. He did his best not to show it. Not since the early days when he'd worked to develop his ability had he had such troubles.

Jarl wiped sweat from his brow and studied their surroundings. They'd reached the correct world. The first world that had shown him what the Crystal did to its surroundings.

William and Ari swore softly at the desolation. It looked worse than Jarl remembered.

Jarl, are you well? Dega stared at him.

That was more difficult than I had expected. The Crystals lend us much power, even for an innate ability. He hated to admit it, even to a Traveler he respected.

Will you be able to transport an entire group of Alfar?

Her concern was well founded.

Jarl sighed. *I brought my rings in case I needed them. It appears I will. I suspect with enough practice I could stretch my own abilities. We do not have that time.*

Dega studied him for another moment before flicking her ears back. She bobbed her head, however, seeming to approve despite her displeasure.

Skin crawling, Jarl pulled the magically insulated pouch out of a pocket and slid his rings on.

After not having worn them for a while, the feeling of power was almost overwhelming. He understood now, more than he had before, why Mages earned their rings one at a time. He put his hand out, leaning on Dega's shoulder. He felt her skin ripple, but she didn't step away until Jarl had his balance again.

"Jarl, are you all right?" Ari asked from her back.

"Yes, a moment of dizziness is all." He cast another small glamour to hide his rings from sight. Jarl straightened, exhilarated at the rush of power that flowed through him. How had he given this up? This was life, this was…he should go home and stop his war on…

Startled, Jarl glanced around. Where had those thoughts come from? He glanced down at his hands. Could the Crystal truly be sentient?

Taking a deep breath Jarl constructed mental barriers to would protect him for the next few hours. Then he'd take the rings off, and hopefully never have to use them again.

Are you ready? Dega turned her head so she looked directly at him.

"Yes."

He glanced at the others and got nods in return. Steeling himself, he gathered the feel of Neuhelm. He recalled not liking it there much. Saga and Orlinza had been harassed there, and overall the place had left a bad feeling in his mind. However, it also had the scent of damp forest, and the feel of life that went with being surrounded by trees. He placed all that firmly in his mind and chose a spot outside the city where they would likely be unnoticed if they appeared.

The Alfar being held in a place everyone knew Jarl had been to before lent power to the theory that this was a trap. It also indicated that his people might not realize the extent of the Travelers' ability to go places.

Jarl shook his head and stopped delaying. William and Ari were giving him concerned frowns. Dega, likely aware of his surface thoughts, had her ears pinned.

Pushing one last niggling thought away—that they'd be close to Ceridwen—he grasped his magic and transported them into a small clearing in the forest near Neuhelm. This time the transition seemed effortless. He clenched his fists when they arrived, reveling in the extra power his rings gave him. It would be so easy.

No.

He almost took them off, but until they were safely away, he couldn't afford to be without their power. He couldn't take the risk that he wouldn't have time to put them on before having to rescue the Alfar. He wouldn't fail them. He wouldn't fail Saga.

Branches snapped nearby and Jarl spun, hands up, ready to defend the others.

Chapter 8

Saga watched Jarl and the others go, ears laid back. She hated letting Jarl out of her sight when he went into danger without her. Stomping the ground, she swished her tail irritably when Orlinza put her hand on Saga's shoulder.

"He will be careful," she tried to reassure Saga.

I know. I don't like it though. Swishing her tail irritably, Saga turned toward the assembled Travelers. *Everyone understands the plan?*

The other Travelers nodded or voiced their assent.

Let's go. Saga led the way into the *Through* and they came out in the same grassy pasture she'd visited the previous day.

They'd debated wearing saddles for the Alfars' comfort and security but decided it would attract far less attention without them.

Not having anything else to do until Jarl arrived with the freed Alfar, they set two members of their herd as sentries and the rest fell to grazing.

∞ ∞ ∞

Jarl reacted before the Vanir who stumbled upon them could. He bound the man with magic and stuck a gag in his mouth. Ari and William glared at Jarl. He ignored them, senses alert for others.

Dega, do you sense anyone?

No. The certainty in her voice relaxed Jarl a fraction.

The man stared at Ari, eyes wide, likely assuming him to be the mage since he was mounted.

Jarl glanced up at Ari and gestured toward the man.

Ari frowned and Jarl shut his eyes for a moment.

Dega, please tell him to be rude and condescending, but to address the guard, not as an enemy but merely as someone who unfortunately startled a mage.

After a moment Ari started and turned his attention to the captured man. He waved his hand in an elaborate flourish and Jarl dropped the gag.

"What, exactly, are you doing out here in the woods at this time of night?"

"Pardon, m'lord." The man bobbed his head since he couldn't otherwise bow. "I'm one of the sentries. Got all those Alfar in there, don't want anything to happen before they're handled."

His smile made Jarl's blood boil.

Ari inclined his head, as if this wasn't a surprise to him. He even managed to handle himself like a lord. Jarl wondered if perhaps he was one.

"Very well," Ari told him.

"Pardon, m'lord, what exactly are *you* doing out here in the woods at this time of night?"

Jarl winced. This guard wasn't dumb, and while he knew he was dealing with a mage, he didn't recognize Ari or trust him. In another time Jarl would have commended the man. Now he'd likely condemned himself. Trying to decide what to do with the solider, Jarl searched for ideas.

"None of your concern." Ari sniffed dismissively.

"Then you won't mind coming with me back to Neuhelm." The soldier straightened, as much as he could, in his bonds.

The man was brave, Jarl would give him that. It was too bad.

Ari raised an eyebrow, as if amused by the man. As he opened his mouth to reply, the sentry's eyes went wide, and he shuddered before going limp.

William stepped out from behind the dead man, bloody knife in his hand. "Don't have time to banter," he grunted. "We had to kill him anyway."

Jarl, shocked, took a moment to collect his thoughts. "Did it not occur to you that I could have taken him someplace where he'd be out of the way?"

"What, and have to fight him some other time." William shrugged. "They've killed plenty of ours."

Clenching his jaw, Jarl kept his retort to himself. William's complete lack of concern worried him more than the actual murder. His own lack of reaction bothered Jarl a little as well.

He shrugged it off and gestured for the others to follow him.

"Remember, Jarl, you're merely a servant," Ari said as they followed.

Jarl didn't answer.

They followed Jarl to the roadway where Ari and Dega rode to the front and Jarl and William trailed along behind, like good servants. He'd considered taking them directly to where the Alfar were located. Everyone had decided that it would attract too much attention if they were noticed. It being late evening was suspicious enough.

The scouts had reported no mages amongst the guards, both at the wall and guarding the Alfar. As long as that stayed consistent, they had a good chance of pulling off the rescue. Inspired by their encounter with the sentry, he considered adding a touch of blue to Ari's uniform, indicating to all that he was a mage. If an enemy mage did appear, it could cause trouble. Most mages were known to other mages, if not by sight, at least by reputation. There weren't so many in the world that they could remain anonymous to one another. To the average guard, however, that would be different. He could always add a touch if they needed it.

The first obstacle was the gate.

Ari rode up to it as if he owned the world. Dega arched her neck and carried herself perfectly as a well-trained saddle horse would.

Jarl and William hung back. Fortunately, Ari's accent wasn't heavy, and he could pass for Vanir in speech. He'd managed to get the arrogant lord aspect down too, and the gate guards gave them little trouble.

Trying not to look too interested in anything as they moved into the city, Jarl still glanced around, making sure that no one paid too much attention to their group.

A few people walked about, despite the late hour. Mostly, Jarl recognized soldiers. Far more than from his last visit. Even if this weren't a trap, they were guarding against trouble. They walked to a local inn as if they were in no particular hurry, dismounted, and loosely tied Dega to the hitching rail. The knot would come lose with no effort on her part. They went inside, secured a room with coin acquired by the scouts and then made excuses about visiting another establishment for their supper, despite the innkeeper's protest that his food was the finest in Neuhelm.

They'd secured their cover story as thoroughly as possible, and slipped into the darkening shadows to go rescue the Alfar.

Dega would keep watch from her station, and join them or escape on her own, depending on what the situation called for.

Leaving her behind, though she wasn't defenseless, made the skin crawl on the back of Jarl's neck. He suspected, more than any other element of their disguise, the bit in Dega's mouth would do more to convince any suspicious person that she was merely a horse.

Ari lead, more experienced at this kind of subterfuge than Jarl, although Jarl knew the city better. They crouched in an alley and Jarl had cast another glamour, causing the shadows to cling to them and blur their outlines. He didn't want to use much magic in case it would be detected, but glamours took little magic and were easy to miss to someone searching for spells.

"Huh, she looks important," Ari said quietly.

Jarl scooted forward, still at a crouch. His jaw dropped, and his heart wrenched. What was Ceridwen doing in Neuhelm.

"Know her?"

"Quiet," Jarl hissed, straining to hear what Ceridwen said to the two men she walked with. Lady Alis trailed along behind, as always.

"I will see they are properly treated," she said.

"Shards," Jarl muttered under his breath.

"What?" William scooted closer.

"That's my betrothed. *Was* my betrothed." Jarl forced the emotion out of his voice and buried it under a wall in his mind.

"Will she be a problem?" William fingered his knife.

"I will kill you if you even think about harming her." Jarl turned the full weight of his glare upon William.

The other man blanched and nodded.

"She freed those other Alfar."

"Could have been bait for the trap." William met Jarl's gaze this time and didn't back down.

He shook his head. "Saga still trusts her, and I trust Saga. Just stay away from her and we'll be fine. I do not believe she'd sound the alarm if she saw the Alfar escaping, not if she could get away with it, at least."

William gave a non-committal grunt and Ari shrugged.

"The way is clear," Ari said a moment later. "Let's go."

Jarl and William followed Ari out into the street. Jarl dropped the glamour and they walked down the middle of the dirt road as if they had nonurgent business. This ruse got them close enough to the holding area, a stockyard, that Jarl could smell the unwashed bodies of many Alfar over the stench of animal feces.

Wrinkling his nose, Jarl took the lead. He'd been here once before, however the yards had been empty at that time. They continued down the dirt road they walked, and he took an alley past one of the stockyard buildings. They'd encounter guards soon, and perhaps William would get to exact more revenge against Jarl's people.

He put that thought out of his mind, recasting the shadow glamour and trying not to breathe in the smell that hung heavy in the narrow, still alley. William and

Ari crept behind Jarl, and they paused frequently, listening.

Jarl's heart raced. He wasn't too worried about defending himself and his companions. He even thought if it came to a straight-up fight, he'd be able to best other mages and escape with the Alfar. It would be messy, but with the added power of his rings, he'd manage. What truly made his heart race was Ceridwen's presence. If she got hurt during the rescue, he'd never forgive himself.

He crept around a corner and paused, crouching. Stones crunched under a booted foot. Waiting, he heard more footsteps.

Ari crouched next to him, hand up for silence, as if the others hadn't heard. Finally, he nodded and gestured for them to move forward. William followed behind, and Jarl's shoulder blades itched. He didn't exactly trust the man, especially after Jarl had threatened him earlier. For now they were on the same mission. Hopefully William remembered that as well.

Pausing at the next junction, Ari put up a hand. William and Jarl both halted. Ari held up two fingers and pointed to their right, before falling back.

"There are two guards. We either need to silence them, or go around," Ari whispered.

"Not many ways around," Jarl replied.

"Can you gag them with magic again?" William drew his knife.

Jarl hesitated. He could. He could even kill them with magic, but even if they were the opponents, and Jarl wasn't quite ready to admit that all his people were his enemy, he couldn't stomach tying someone up simply to be knifed in the back.

"They're the enemy, *m'lord*." William's voice dripped with derision.

"How would you feel if some trussed you up with magic then stabbed you?" Jarl retorted.

William didn't reply, simply glared back.

"Let me handle it," Jarl growled. He deepened the glamour that obscured his form and crept around the corner before either man could object. He would knock them out, then make sure William didn't stab them on the way. The spell Jarl knew would keep them out for hours. He simply had to touch them.

Creeping down the ally, conscious of William and Ari watching him, Jarl approached the guards. Magic hid him from sight, but he had forgotten to muffle his footsteps. They turned his direction, and Jarl froze. *Shards*.

Chapter 9

The guards' gazes swept over him and kept scanning. They weren't close enough to touch, not yet. Cursing silently, heart thudding in his chest, he waited for them to study the alley and prayed he'd made his glamour heavy enough. He was loath to use too much magic, not while his presence was still a secret.

Finally, the two guards looked at each other then went back to idly scanning for threats.

Not letting himself relax, Jarl continued creeping forward until he could touch both men. Preparing the spell to knock them out, he grabbed both on their bare arms at the same time. One got out a quiet gasp before both fell unconscious. Jarl tried to ease their falls and left them slumped on the ground.

Ari and William joined him. "How long will they be out?" Ari felt one of their necks for a pulse.

"A couple of hours," Jarl answered.

"Let's drag them out of the main alley." Ari grabbed one, William grabbed another, and they pulled them out of sight.

They returned moments later, and Jarl had to hope the guards were still alive. He didn't ask.

They continued creeping along until they came out from between the stockyard buildings. There they crouched in the shadows and watched.

The ache in Jarl's back from the crouching was nothing compared to the ache in his heart at the conditions the Alfar were currently forced to endure. They'd never been treated well to begin with. Even the lowest of animals were treated better than what he saw before him. It was difficult to tell anything about the Alfar beyond the mud that coated them, other that their clothing was in rags, they had no sanitation, no space, and no food. Gaunt frames leaned against the walls of the pen, and other gaunt frames leaned against those bodies. He knew most, if not all, were still alive by the way they stood instead of lay crumpled on the ground. That was all he could tell.

He almost dashed forward to transport them all away when Ceridwen stormed into view.

"This is deplorable. How can you keep them in such conditions?" She rounded on the man standing next to her, hands curled into fists.

For a moment, Jarl's heart swelled with pride at the way she tried to take charge.

"Orders from the high mages, m'lady. No choice. Besides, they're to die tomorrow. What does it matter how they're treated?"

Jarl could feel the force of Ceridwen's glare from his location, and he wasn't even bearing the brunt of it.

The man she addressed wilted but shook his head. "Nothing to be done. Can't go against the high mages."

Ceridwen gave a curt nod and spun on her heels.

Jarl breathed a sigh of relief when she stalked away. They gave Ceridwen and the others a few more moments, then, alert for guards, they crept forward.

The Alfar saw them more quickly than a human would have. Jarl didn't drop the glamour, just got close enough that he could enclose the entire pen with his Farer ability. For as many Alfar as there were, they were in a tiny space, which made his job easier.

They stared with weary eyes. Jarl ignored them. They'd figure out what was going on soon enough.

He gathered the feel of the world they were supposed to go to and reached. Nothing.

"Let's go," Ari said tightly.

"I'm trying," Jarl growled.

Both he and William stared at Jarl suspiciously.

"There's something blocking my ability. I've heard of such wards. I didn't expect it. It's not common knowledge." Jarl gritted his teeth. Of course, his parents would have had wards set against easy transportation.

"Can you take the ward down?"

"It'll take time." Jarl stared at the captive Alfar. They could see through his glamours and the faint flicker of hope he saw in their eyes died at his words.

"Shards," Jarl muttered. "Keep an eye out. I'll see what I can do." He would have to use more magic than he had wanted to. It would attract attention, so he'd have to be fast.

He dropped into his magesight and looked at the wards. They were twisty and complicated. He could unravel them, with enough time. Shards. They'd set alarms, too. Those had to go first.

Dropping the glamours, he couldn't concentrate on both tasks, Jarl set to unraveling the alarms.

"Did he just…?" William said.

"Yes. Jarl, what are you doing," Ari hissed.

"You wanted the wards down, I need to concentrate," Jarl said through gritted teeth. "They're going to notice my magic use anyway."

Ari cursed and drew his sword. William carried a long knife along with his daggers. Jarl hoped he wouldn't need the curved blade he carried. He'd far rather fight from Saga's back.

"Someone is coming," one of the Alfar said. "They sent word from the other side of the pen."

Jarl cursed, gave up caution, and tore at the wards with all the magical power he could muster. He felt the remaining alarm ward blare and winced. "They'll come soon. Be ready."

Sweat ran down his temples as he pulled the wards apart with brute strength. The seductive call of the Crystal's power thrummed through him, and he had to ignore it, fully concentrating on his magic.

He almost didn't notice when Ari and William engaged the first guards. The shouts soon caught his attention. Jarl drew his sword, dividing his attention between the magic and defending himself.

Parry, tear at the wards, thrust, dodge, more magic. He couldn't even spare his attention enough to cast a magical attack. He had to get those wards down, or all was lost.

His head ached as he pounded against the threads of energy that kept them trapped on this world. He could take a few steps away and escape, but that would leave the others to certain death.

Dega!

I am coming.

Moments later the Traveler appeared at his side and struck out at the increasingly large number of guards. That gave him enough of a reprieve that he could refocus on his task.

Ari and William were good, and with their backs protected, they were able to keep many of the guards at bay. Dega held Jarl's side while he worked, though she wasn't armored. He worried for her safety.

Of course, neither were Ari or William.

Jarl saw Ari fall, and not truly thinking about what he did, he darted forward to cover both men while William helped Ari rise.

"You have to get us out of here!" William shouted.

"Working on it," Jarl snarled. Desperately he threw pure energy at the men assaulting them, flinging them all back a pace. Then he turned away from the fight, and throwing his arms up, shoved everything he had at breaking the ward.

It shattered.

Jarl staggered back and cried out as something bit into his side.

Collapsing, he barely kept hold of his sword and twisted, blocking a thrust at the last moment.

Two white fletched arrows struck the ground on either side of him, and the man who attacked him jumped back in shock.

Jarl wasn't sure whom the arrows had been intended for, but he took the reprieve and called his Farer magic to him. Grabbing the Alfar, William, and Ari with his power, he pulled them all away from the fight.

For a moment, the change from dark, torch-lit night to late evening sun was more than Jarl could handle. Pain shot through his side and he collapsed to the ground.

"Go!" William yelled at the Alfar. "Get on one of the Travelers. We have to go now!"

Jarl, are you okay? Saga appeared next to him.

He grabbed her mane and let her haul him to his feet. "I'm fine." He wasn't, but they didn't have time to deal with it. "We have to go. They'll follow us." Jarl struggled to Saga's back. The Alfar were mounted or helping each other mount, and as soon as the

77

Travelers had as many as they could take, two or three at a time, they vanished.

Jarl and Saga waited until the others had all scattered, then they entered the *Through*, bouncing off worlds.

Beginning to feel faint, Jarl wished the ride would end soon. He needed to rest. The magic had taken a lot out of him, and his side ached, but there would be time to deal with that later.

His vision blackened, and he shook his head when they reached the Travelers' home world. The others would be arriving here and at other settlements with their Alfar passengers. If they had done their jobs right, everyone would make it safely.

You're injured.

"It's not bad," Jarl said as he slumped a little on Saga's back.

She trotted over to a group of the others.

Jarl groaned.

He was about to slide from the Traveler's back and ask Orlinza to help him, when Dance appeared in the field screaming frantically.

They have Ima!

"How can they have Ima?" Jarl looked around for the white-haired Alfar. She was nowhere to be seen. She hadn't been assigned to any raid.

Aderyn ran up to Jarl. "We sent other rescue missions at the same time as yours. We didn't think they'd let the other Alfar live once you rescued your group."

"And you didn't tell me?" Jarl's rage flared, driving away the pain from his wound.

"You didn't need to know." She had the grace to look away.

Grinding his teeth, Jarl clenched Saga's mane. "Where was she?"

"The rescue group outside of the main city. About a league from the walls. There's a small village there, easily reinforced from the main city," Aderyn said hastily.

"I know it." Jarl squeezed his legs and Saga spun. They didn't need to confer to know what both would want to do. She leapt into a gallop, and Jarl used his magic to transport them to the small town.

They burst out of the fog his power generated straight into a startled group of guards. They cried out and fell back.

There. Saga spotted Ima. She knelt with her hands bound behind her. Two mages stood before her and Ima screamed when one touched her arm. He used a spell Jarl knew of but had never performed. It was only good for torture. Saga took over, stepping into the *Through* at a full gallop and appearing behind Ima.

Jarl, with no time for finesse, blasted the two mages backward with pure energy. They fell back as Jarl slid off Saga's back and grabbed Ima.

It was all he could do to throw her on Saga's back. His muscles gave out and he fell before he could remount.

The mages recovered and began chanting the spell for the stun net that would capture Saga.

"Go!"

He struggled to his knees.

I'm not leaving you!

I can get out on my own. Run, now!

Saga obeyed, vanishing.

Jarl lurched to his feet and tried to escape with his own abilities, but the mages hit him with the net. Crying out, he fought to remain conscious, tried to fight the stun net. His energy failed, and his vision went black.

Chapter 10

Saga bounced through worlds as quickly as she could, hardly daring to breathe as she flickered in and out of the *Through*. Something had happened to Jarl just before she'd left with Ima. The poor Alfar clung to Saga's back with her legs, her arms still tied behind her. Saga could feel her tremble and judged that she had gone far enough. She focused on the home world and dashed out of the *Through*.

Rainer galloped to her side, unseating Ima in his haste to make sure she was okay. She cried out as she slid from Saga's back.

Aderyn and Orlinza arrived with a few others after a moment and helped Ima stand.

I'm sorry! Rainier swished his tail, agitated.

"It's okay, Ranier." Ima stretched her hands and arms as soon as Aderyn cut them free. Then she threw her arms around the distraught Traveler's neck. "I'm not mad and I'm not hurt."

"Jarl?" Orlinza pressed her hands against Saga's side, her eyes are wide with worry.

They hit him before he could escape. Saga couldn't continue.

"Crystal Shards," Aderyn cursed. "We need that boy."

Saga tossed her head. *They will not kill him, at least.* Laying her ears back, she tried to come up with a plan. Some way to save him that wouldn't get more people killed. As much as she wanted to rush off and try to rescue him, he'd be too well guarded by now, and if the smell of blood from her tack was any indication, he was more badly injured than he'd allowed. At least with the Vanir he'd receive magical healing. For now, he was likely better off.

She told herself that, but she didn't believe it.

Orlinza put her hand on Saga's shoulder. "We will get him back, and you're right. They won't hurt him. Not right away, at least."

Orlinza's words weren't nearly as comforting as Saga guessed the Alfar had intended. She nodded anyway.

"We managed to rescue many of the captive Alfar. We didn't get them all. I'm not sure we could have. The other team got almost everyone out. Ima's group had the hardest task and even they got out nearly half." Orlinza's cheer sounded forced.

So many of her people killed, all because of a war almost no one remembered. No, Saga thought shaking her head, the deaths were all because of the Crystal parasite. Now, more than ever, Saga wanted it destroyed.

∞ ∞ ∞

Jarl's temples throbbed and his eyes felt like they might explode out of their sockets. When he turned his head slightly, the wave of nausea almost made him lose what was left of his long distant dinner. He didn't dare open his eyes. He tried to listen through the pounding in his ears.

He couldn't hear much, but from the chill air he thought they had either dumped him in the dungeon or transported him to someplace in the Mountains.

82

At that moment, he didn't care where he was. He simply wanted the pain to stop. After a time, the ache receded a little, and the rest of the aches made themselves known, most notably the pain in his side. He thought someone might have bound it, to stop the bleeding, or he likely wouldn't have woken at all. No one had healed him.

That by itself made him think he was in the dungeons. Obviously, his parents were furious with him. Rightly so.

"Is he awake yet?"

For a moment, Jarl thought he imagined his mother's voice.

"We're not sure, M'lady Nessa," someone else said.

It had been his mother. For a moment, Jarl was glad. She'd fix everything. Then pain lanced through him, and the reality of his situation hit home, again. He wasn't ten anymore. He'd made his choice, and his choice had taken him far away from anything his parents would approve of. She couldn't fix anything. Well, maybe she'd heal him, but then again, maybe they felt he deserved his pain.

"Let me in," Nessa said.

"Yes, m'lady."

Jarl heard a lock turn and the creak of metal hinges. The dungeon then. He wasn't completely surprised.

"Jarl?" The tenderness in his mother's voice almost brought tears to his eyes, but he heard a hint of strident fear too that worried him.

He groaned. It was all he could manage.

"Oh, for Egal's sake."

He heard a rustle from her robes as she knelt. He winced when she put a hand on him. Being touched hurt.

Nessa muttered under her breath then a blast of cool, healing energy roared through him. Jarl's back arched and he cried out. Healing hurt, and left him feeling drained, but slowly the ache faded. He pried his eyes open and rubbed at the crust that had glued them shut.

"You're covered in blood." Nessa's statement contained depths of accusation Jarl wasn't prepared to deal with, so he said nothing.

"Oh, Jarl, how could you?"

"How could you, Mother?" His voice sounded thready and as weak as he felt.

"Excuse me?"

"You attempted to have my best friend killed. She'd done nothing to deserve that." The accusation was difficult, even with the anger that he felt. He and his parents had never truly fought, and he wasn't practiced at being angry with them.

"We did what we had to. You were in danger because of her." Nessa's voice remained neutral.

"No. I was not. Not until you forced us to leave this world."

"I did not force you to do anything. Jarl, you are the heir. If you work with us, everything can be forgiven. Come home."

"No." The word tore at his throat, but he had to say it. What else could he do?

"I do suspect we won't convince you by leaving you in the dungeons. I will see what can be arranged." Her voice sharpened and her eyes narrowed as she stood and turned away. "We love you, Jarl. You must remember that. We only want what is best for you."

He couldn't bring himself to reply as she walked out. He let weariness pull his eyes shut and sank back to sleep.

∞ ∞ ∞

The next time Jarl woke, his father stood over him. He'd thought facing his mother was difficult. His father was far worse. Geraint stood with his arms crossed, watching Jarl.

His expression lightened when Jarl met his eyes, however.

"How do you feel, son?"

Jarl shrugged and was grateful to discover the motion didn't hurt. "Reasonably well, considering."

"Your mother does not wish to see you locked in the dungeon, and..." he hesitated. "Neither do I. If I thought you would give an oath not to attempt to escape, I would accept it, but I do not believe you would give one. We give you leave of the castle. You must stay inside and a guard will remain with you."

Jarl frowned. "What is to prevent me from simply leaving?"

His father gestured at his wrist.

Lifting his arm, Jarl saw a thin metal band with no obvious seam wrapped tightly around his wrist. It was gold and looked like jewelry. On closer inspection he could see faint runes stamped into the metal. He'd heard of devices that blocked magic. He'd never seen one. He also noted that his rings were gone. That didn't bother him nearly as much.

Raising his eyebrows, he tried to perform a minor glamour. The metal burned his skin and he couldn't touch the magic at all.

Wincing, he glanced at his father. He didn't let any of his emotions show, and truthfully, he didn't know how he felt. He felt betrayed, though he had no right to that emotion. He also felt resigned. He'd never manage to escape…however, this was also an opportunity. He was confined indoors, but, the library was here. At the very least he could attempt some research until he figured out what he would do next.

"It is not widely known outside of the mage community what has occurred. I expect it to remain that way." Geraint crossed his arms.

Jarl nodded.

"Good. Get up then. I'll escort you to your rooms. You need to clean up. Stay there until someone comes for you." He turned and Jarl stared at his broad back for a moment before he swung his feet over the edge of the hard cot he laid on. He supposed he'd gotten that much because of who he was. Most would have had nothing but the floor.

He stood slowly, feeling weak. Hopefully, someone would bring food in his rooms.

∞ ∞ ∞

Conor came with food after Jarl had a chance to clean up. His fine clothing felt strange against his skin after months of wearing Tomas's. He had chosen work clothes, not interested in any finery.

Conor had dressed with his normal care, and Jarl almost felt shabby in comparison. Or perhaps that was simply mental and related to the way Jarl felt.

"Hello." Conor set the platters on Jarl's table. "We thought you might be hungry."

Hungry was an understatement, but Jarl didn't want to say more than he had to. He didn't want to become too comfortable here. It would be too easy to give in. Too easy to fall into old patterns and pretend everything was all right.

"Are you my guard for the day?" Jarl tried to keep his tone to idle curiosity. A hint of bitterness crept in.

Conor sighed. "I'm your friend, Jarl. I'm here so that you don't have to be followed around by a guard. So, what would you like to do today? After you eat. I have no other duties."

A friendly guard was still a guard, Jarl thought but didn't say anything aloud. "I'd like to go to the library. I must do some research."

Conor set out plates. "You may not be hungry, but I am."

Reluctantly, Jarl sat across from Conor and picked up a roll. The food was far better than they had on the Travelers' home world and, though he didn't want to, he resolved to enjoy it while he could.

Chapter 11

Research in the library proved more challenging than Jarl had expected. With Conor standing over his shoulder, figuratively at least, he couldn't make his interest in the origins of the Crystal known. So, instead he pulled as many random history books at a time as he could carry, trying to include at least one that contained information on the Crystal, each arm full. It would take much longer this way, especially since he didn't dare use help from the librarian either, but he had some time.

After several hours, Conor looked up from his own stack of books. Magical theory that Jarl had barely glanced at before going back to the histories.

"What are you looking for?"

Jarl shrugged. "Nothing in particular."

Conor leaned back and watched while Jarl read. This was a book that interested him. It covered the early use of the Crystal to fuel magic. It contained essays on early experimentation and even mentioned that the scholars and mages who studied it suspected it had come from another world, as they could find no evidence that it had been long on this one.

They discovered that it harmed the environment and made the choice to regulate it to the southern continent where fewer people lived. It also mentioned Dvergr caves and their insistence that the Crystal not be brought there.

Interesting. There had been Dvergr on this world at one point.

Not wanting to show too much interest in this tome, he made note of the title and set it aside for a history of the Stonespyne Mountains, where the Dvergr had once lived. That could also have important information.

He wished he could speak to the dragon again to see if he had any more information to share. Once he escaped, he would make an effort to do so.

He simply had to believe that if he could find the origins of the Crystal he could destroy it and that action would destroy all the growths.

"Jarl, I believe Ceridwen is here to see you," Conor said.

Surprised, Jarl glanced up and tried to school his face to impassiveness. It was hard. He wanted to smile and wrap his arms around her. She did smile when she saw him, though it was somewhat guarded.

"I'll just be over there." Conor pointed to the library entrance. The only way in or out of the enormous room.

Jarl stood as Ceridwen approached. She wore the simple sky-blue gown he'd first seen her in. It made her brown eyes glow like burnished amber even in the artificial mage lights that illuminated the library.

"Hello," she said softly.

"Hi." He offered his arm, and she slid her hand through it. The warmth of her hand resting on his arm almost undid him. His mage training had prepared him to control his emotions and he kept his feelings in check.

"Shall we walk?" She gestured toward the stacks. She wore the arrow earrings he'd given her at their betrothal. They glinted in the low mage light and the sight made his heart clench.

They could get lost in the maze of books for a time. He nodded and they headed deep into the maze. Mage lights lit the rows. The shadows seemed a physical presence along with the slightly musty scent of the books themselves. Dry, old, solid, yet also fragile.

"I was afraid of the deeper parts of the library when I was young," he said after they'd walked in silence for a time.

Ceridwen looked around them. "I can imagine."

He sighed. "I'm sorry."

She glanced over her shoulder. "Can we be overheard?"

"There is no one else around, but I can't be certain that magical eavesdropping won't occur."

Frowning, Ceridwen glanced at him and tilted her head.

He held up his left arm. "They've blocked my magic, for now." Smiling ruefully, he continued. "It's as if they don't trust me."

Squeezing his arm with her hand she cast one more look around before shrugging. "It is a risk we will have to take then. They want me to convince you to return. To give up on the Travelers and their conflict with the Vanir."

"Ceridwen, the Crystal is evil. It's controlling my people. It must be destroyed," he whispered.

"So Saga said."

"You don't believe me?"

"I'm not a mage, Jarl. I know very little of your ways and it isn't my place to say." Her sad voice tore at his heart.

"I took off my rings for several weeks, only putting them back on recently because I needed the extra power. When I did, I heard a voice, oily, quiet, trying to sink into my mind. It said I should return to my world, give up on the Travelers, similar things to what my parents told you to say to me. It also talked about power, as if it tried to seduce me back with magical power. I didn't believe it anything more than a parasite until then. I'm convinced now."

Ceridwen stopped walking and turned to stare at him. After a moment, she nodded. "Then I will believe as well. What can you do?"

He hated keeping anything from her, he couldn't tell Ceridwen his plan. Even if she was fully devoted to him, it wouldn't be safe for her to know. "I don't know."

She dropped her gaze for a moment before resuming their walk.

"When we thought you were dead, your parents spoke of pairing me with Conor. They believe I will make a fine ruler of Vanaheim, and he is next in line for the throne." She glanced at him, perhaps to gage his reaction.

Suppressing a flash of jealousy, Jarl tried to unknot his shoulders. "What do you think of that plan?"

"It is a wise move, politically."

Jarl smiled. "Conor is a decent man. He would treat you well."

She sighed. "Yes, I suppose that is true. I had thought I would get to marry for love after all, when we were betrothed. At least I will get a decent man and a good position."

"I'm sorry," he found himself apologizing again. "I don't know if it helps, but I miss you terribly."

Ceridwen ducked her head, but finally she looked up smiling, eyes glistening with unshed tears. "I wish I could ask you to give up your quest for me. To return to me and bring change once you are ruler, but if you did that, the things I love about you would be diminished. So, I won't. I will ask you to be careful, and if I can help you escape I will."

Jarl turned toward Ceridwen, putting his hands on her shoulders, though he wanted to pull her close. "I would ask you to leave with me, but our people need you, and I wouldn't ask you not to be true to them. I didn't have a chance to say, but I love you, Ceridwen."

"And I you," she whispered, tears glistening in her eyes.

Jarl felt his eyes burn as well. He kept his tears in check. If they both started sobbing, they might never stop.

"Please remember, no matter what, I'm trying to help our people."

Ceridwen stepped forward and hugged him. He put his arms around her and squeezed. She rested her head against his shoulder, and he inhaled her scent, floral with a hint of her forest home.

"I will miss you," Jarl said.

"And I you. I will return home today, unless you think I can assist you here."

"No." Jarl released her. "I want you to be safe. Thank you."

She stepped back, wiping at her eyes. "I will remember that you care for us, Jarl. And, if you do succeed in your mission, perhaps we will meet again under better circumstances."

He couldn't reply to that, his throat feeling thick, so he offered his arm and led her out of the book-maze and schooled his features. He didn't want to hand her off to Conor, but it was the best thing for her. Conor's position would protect her from any potential backlash, and she would rule Vanaheim well in the future. He just hoped he didn't destroy what she loved. He wanted to save his world, not ruin it.

She left him near the table where his books were stacked and headed to where Conor waited. She spoke with him briefly, glanced back at Jarl one last time, and then was gone.

Perhaps they'd meet again, perhaps not, but for now it was better this way. Jarl repeated that to himself a few times, hoping he'd believe it eventually. He felt like he ripped his heart from his chest and stomped on it. Perhaps she felt the same.

Chapter 12

Saga paced around the edge of the clearing, tail swishing and ears pinned.

"Saga, there is nothing we can do while he's in the city." Orlinza walked near her, trying to keep up while they talked.

Slowing, Saga swiveled her ears toward Orlinza. Her friend was correct. She didn't like it.

"If he could escape on his own, he would have done so by now. Perhaps they blocked his magic."

We must do something.

"I agree. What?"

Saga lashed her tail. *I don't know. I can't just stand here. I'm going somewhere.*

"Where?"

I don't know! Saga immediately felt bad. Orlinza just patted her shoulder.

"Saga, go Travel somewhere. Go look for Dvergr, or dragons, or something. Come back in a couple of hours."

I will go talk to Tala.

"I'll see you soon, Saga."

The Traveler nodded and headed into the clearing and then into the *Through*. After bouncing off a few worlds, she came out on the dragons' world.

Tala, are you there?

I am, Saga. What can I do for you?

They have Jarl. I don't know what to do.

The dragon must have known what Saga meant, or she had abilities like the Travelers to perceive surface thoughts because she didn't question Saga.

Your friend is resourceful.

Yes, but the Vanier are powerful, and they are not happy with him.

Does he also not have friends on that world? Someone will help him escape. You must trust your friend.

Saga lashed her tail and flattened her ears. Tala was right, but Saga was so used to being there to help her friend.

What could you do to make his situation better?

Find the source of the Crystal and destroy it. Saga aimed a kick at crumbled rock as if she could simply destroy it.

If only it were that easy, Tala said.

Saga nodded agreement.

What else can you do?

There wasn't a lot, Saga knew. She already had people working on plans to fight the Crystal using the information they already had.

Be ready if he does need help and can somehow signal me?

Yes. Anything else?

Saga sighed in imitation of the humans she had grown up with. *No.*

You will have to trust Jarl to get out of this without your help. Your capture would make things worse.

I know. Saga grunted in annoyance and flicked her tail again. *Can it be done, Tala?*

Can what be done?

Can we really defeat the Vanier? Destroy the Crystal?

All things can be done, Saga. I believe you and Jarl have a better chance than most at accomplishing that goal. If we are ever truly going to have peace, the Crystal must be destroyed. You've convinced Jarl, and that was probably the hardest task. The rest will just take time.

We don't have time. Saga paced, agitated.

Saga, I would like to see this done quickly as well. Unfortunately, it will take the time it needs to take, and until then, those who can, will fight.

Yet again, Saga knew the dragon was correct, but she didn't like it.

You need to remain confident. The others look to you, and to Jarl even if they don't want to. As long as the two of you believe it can be done, the others will follow and you will accomplish your goals.

Saga perked her ears forward. That, at least, was something she could do. Continue to make sure the others believed. And she would continue to watch for Jarl. Any signal or sign that he might need help and she would go to him. While she did not want to return to Vanaheim, she would do so to rescue her friend.

Tala, thank you.

Of course, Saga. Thank you. Now go. And someday return and help dragons return to our world.

What if it takes too long?

Saga, the dragon eggs have all the time in the world. Complete your quest, and then warm them. Our kind learn in the shell, and the secrets of the dragons were whispered to them long before their dams died from the parasite. They will know what to do upon waking. There is no hurry in that regard. And if you do not defeat the Crystal in your lifetime, tell another until we can once again fly these skies.

Thank you again, Tala. I won't forget. I go now to watch for Jarl, and to trust him to escape without me.

The Traveler felt the dragon's mind brush across hers in a comforting mental embrace before the contact faded.

She trotted into the *Through* and headed for home.

Chapter 13

Jarl, engrossed in the history book he read, jumped when someone touched his arm.

"Jarl, your parents want to talk to you," Connor said.

He put the book down, making a note of which one it was. There was some promising information about the source of the Crystal in it that he wanted to explore further. Not saying anything, he got up and followed Conor. He found he really didn't have much to say to his friend, and Conor hadn't made much effort at conversation.

They hurried through the blue carpeted hallways until they reached Geraint and Nessa's private wing. Jarl had never really noted the opulence before. After living in a nicely built but rough cabin, the hand-carved doors with the family crest of a griffin and the Crystal seemed beautiful, but over the top. The decorations and paintings in the hallways were nice, however he had grown used to a simpler way. He could get used to this again, he was sure. He would rather have his friend, than all the luxuries in the world.

Conor opened the door for him. "I'll be out here," he said.

Remembering a hint of his old arrogance, he didn't thank Conor for opening the door for him. He almost felt bad about it, but wasn't even sure Conor would notice.

"Hello, Mother. Father," Jarl said as he came into their sitting room.

As usual, Nessa sat near the fire, an open book on the table in front of her. Her formal robes draped her in blue velvet. Her blonde hair, normally pulled back into a tight bun or other controlled hairstyle, fell to her elbows and looked almost disheveled. Her typically flawless skin seemed stretched somehow, tired, and shadows collected under eyes that gleamed with a strange fever.

Jarl shivered and looked away. His father wore his normal sturdy breeches and a fine shirt covered with a vest, all in shades of blue. He had a few more streaks of gray in his dark curls, and a few more creases on his face. He stood near Nessa with his arms crossed.

"You wanted to see me?"

"Jarl, you must stop this nonsense," Nessa said.

"What nonsense?" Uninvited, he took a seat anyway.

"Your obsession with the Travelers. They're dangerous. They're our enemy, along with the Alfar." Nessa sounded so reasonable as if she believed it with all her heart.

"You know, Mother, the Travelers simply don't want to be enslaved. The Alfar just want to be treated decently, and well, they're rather against being slaves, too. We're the enemy, not them." Jarl knew he was treading a fine line between angering his parents so badly they did something drastic and trying to talk reason into them. He found he just didn't care anymore.

His parents stared at him for a moment before Geraint spoke, voice low. "Jarl, that is quite enough."

100

Perhaps he had already crossed the line a while ago.

"We never should have let that Traveler live and become your friend." Nessa shook her head. "This is all our fault."

"Yes, it is your fault." Jarl stood, voice rising. "If you hadn't tried to kill her for no reason, maybe we wouldn't be having this conversation right now. She was loyal to us, to you. You drove her away and allowed her to see that what the others had told her was true. She didn't believe them until you tried to have her killed."

"Jarl," his father said, warning in his voice.

"No, you have to listen. They just wanted to be left alone. We're the ones who started enslaving them."

"And now they try to destroy our source of power," Nessa said.

Jarl hadn't planned on bringing the Crystal into this at all, but since they had, he would, too. "The Crystal, yes, it gives us more power. It's also controlling us. It's a parasite that destroys the environment and controls anyone who uses it. Do you want to know what happened after I put my rings back on?" He plowed ahead before they could answer. "I hadn't worn them in weeks, and when I put them back on my fingers, I could hear whispers in the back of my mind, telling me things that I had come to learn weren't true."

Geraint and Nessa exchanged a glance with each other. It was clear they weren't considering his words. Perhaps the Crystal had recognized the danger Jarl posed, perhaps his parents didn't need any encouragement from it.

"You leave us no choice, Jarl. You're to be confined to your quarters until we can determine what to do with you. Conor will continue to bring you meals. Otherwise you'll have no contact with the outside world," Geraint said.

Nessa pinched her lips tightly together before nodding. "You must give up these fictions, Jarl."

He didn't reply, simply turned and left the room before they could order him to do so. He shoved their double doors open and headed for his room.

Conor pushed off from the wall he leaned on and followed. "I take it that didn't go well?"

Jarl glanced at his friend, arched his eyebrows, and shrugged. He didn't have anything else to say, and he was already formulating some sort of escape plan. He wasn't sure what he could do without his magic, but he would think of something. Something from his childhood would come to him and he would remember a way out. He had to find a way to escape before Saga came and tried to rescue him. He knew she would eventually, and he didn't want her in that sort of danger.

Jarl pushed open the door to his rooms and shut them in Conor's face. Not the friendliest thing. The low, seething anger he'd felt since his capture was building and he didn't care who knew it anymore. His life here was truly over, not that he hadn't known that before.

Now he just had to get out of here.

If his father hadn't already sealed his room magically, he would soon, so Jarl didn't even try the main doors, and he stayed away from the window. The other obvious escape route. They would seal that as well, he was sure, and they were too high up in the keep for him to get out that way unless he got truly desperate.

His best bet was getting the bracelet off and use his magical abilities to get him off Vanaheim.

From what he remembered, the magical blocking spell was something like a ward. With no magic, he had no way to unravel a ward. Jarl frowned and wondered if it blocked his mage sight.

Unfocusing his eyes, he called upon his extra senses, and to his surprise the threads of magic appeared around him. It was much harder than normal, and pressure built behind his eyes that threatened to turn into a raging headache, but he could see. The webs that cut him off from the energies in the environment weren't something he could even hope to reach. He had innate powers, too, and he could still feel that magic. Maybe, if he were very careful, he could touch...

He woke sometime later, sprawled on his face on the floor with a raging headache. So that approach wasn't going to work. Sighing, Jarl climbed into his bed fully dressed and tried to think.

Chapter 14

"Jarl?"

Jarl snapped his eyes open and glanced around his room. Conor stood in the entrance to the bedchamber, shadows from the moonlight playing across his face.

"Are you okay?"

"Yes. What do you want?" The last was a bit short. Jarl still couldn't bring himself to care.

"Come on, I'm getting you out of here."

"What?"

"You heard me. If you don't give in, they'll tell everyone you were killed by the rebels. They'll leave you stuck in here for the rest of your life."

"You don't think I'll manage to escape eventually?" Jarl sat up and swung his legs over the edge of his bed."

Conor smiled. "Probably. But that will also occur to your parents. They may do worse to you than just block your ability to use magic. I'll get you out of here, and you can go back to your friends, or hide, or whatever you're going to do. One time offer, I won't help you again."

Jarl considered his friend. "Why?"

"You're my friend." Conor said it like that should have been obvious. Maybe he was right.

Jarl hesitated. This could be a trap, but what choice did he have? He hadn't managed to come up with an escape plan yet, and his friend was offering him a way out. "Okay, what's the plan?"

"We're walking out. I'm a mage, remember? I can disguise you."

"And when my parents find out?"

Conor shrugged. "I'm not that worried about it. If they get mad and disown me too, I guess I'll come find you and we can hang out in exile together."

It wasn't that simple, but Jarl wasn't about to argue. He had a much better chance of getting away from Conor than he did from his parents.

"You don't want to be the heir?" Jarl twisted his lips in an attempt at a smile. It didn't work.

"Shards, Jarl, with you out of the way I get the throne and Ceridwen. I can't hardly lose as long as your parents forgive me for letting you escape."

Jarl winced, but there was no excitement in Conor's voice, more resignation.

"You take care of her," he said quietly.

"I will."

"Good, then let's get out of here." Jarl glanced about his room for anything he might want to bring along, but there was nothing. All of Saga's things had already been removed, and he wanted nothing of his own.

Conor cast a glamor over him then led the way to the main room of his suite. After a quick glance outside, Conor gestured for him to follow.

Jarl followed into the hallway where Lady Ailis slipped in behind them. Conor gestured for Jarl to walk up next to him.

Suspiciously, Jarl glanced at his friend.

"Don't ask," Conor whispered, a grin on his face. "Besides, you're close to the same size. Just don't talk."

Jarl supposed if he had to be disguised as someone, his former fiancée wasn't a bad person to be disguised as.

They made it down to the courtyard with no issues, and Conor led the way to the stable where grooms waited with Conor, Ceridwen, and Lady Ailis' horse. Fortunately, they hadn't tacked the women's horses for sidesaddle, which Ceridwen sometimes rode. Jarl might not have been able to fake that convincingly.

Conor, smirking ever so slightly, helped Jarl mount Ceridwen's horse. Jarl wanted to quip back, but he kept his mouth shut.

Lady Ailis mounted and then Conor climbed on his own gelding. Ceridwen's horse twisted her head around to look up at him, nostrils flared. Clearly, she was confused as to who was actually on her back, but the horse was well trained and moved off at a light touch of Jarl's heel.

The grooms bowed and went back into the stable. No one spoke as they rode toward the gates in the wall that surrounded the castle. The guards recognized Conor and opened the door for him and bowed. Jarl couldn't help remembering some of their escapades as children, trying to sneak past guards, actually sneaking past guards, sometimes getting caught, sometimes not.

It was the last time they'd ever sneak around together.

The capitol city never really slept and though it was later, it wasn't so late that people didn't move about in the streets. They all gave way to the small group of riders and Jarl tried to take in his birthplace for the last time.

He found that, without Saga's commentary and his knowledge that everything was built on essentially a lie, the city seemed flat. Not nearly as real as the small hut he lived in on the Travelers' home world.

Once they reached the bridge on the edge of town, Conor broke into a canter, and the other horses followed.

They rode far out into the countryside, alternating between trotting and cantering until they came near the small farmstead where Jarl and Saga had been kidnapped all those years ago.

"Here's where you get off," Conor said. He dismounted, his horse standing quietly when he left him by Lady Ailis' horse.

Jarl dismounted and held up his wrist. Conor pursed his lips before putting his hands on the band that blocked Jarl's magic.

After a moment it opened and fell away in Conor's hands.

The return of his magical senses made him feel whole again. He hadn't realized how much he depended on them to experience the world around him, even when he wasn't actively using magic.

He managed not to show much reaction. "Thank you, Conor. Thank you, Lady Ailis."

She smiled. "Of course, Jarl. Ceridwen told me to send her love as well. She will miss you."

Jarl smiled. "Please return the same message."

She nodded.

Conor held open his arms, and Jarl hugged him. "Thank you," he said again.

"Of course, Jarl. Now don't get caught again. I will miss you. I guess I don't want to see you again, unless somehow this whole mess is resolved." Conor's voice stayed even. Jarl knew his friend well enough to sense the emotions underneath. "I'd be more than happy to step back into my place as your most trusted advisor." He mounted his horse and Jarl handed him the reins of Ceridwen's horse.

"Let's hope we can figure it out."

"Let's hope." Conor rode away with Lady Ailis following.

Jarl watched for a moment before he reached for his Farer abilities. It was time to go home. After he visited a few other worlds to throw off any potential pursuit.

Chapter 15

I can't wait any longer. I must rescue him.

"Saga, you can't. You'll be captured, too." Orlinza put her hand on Saga's shoulder.

Saga tossed her head, sending her black mane flying.

"I know it's hard, but we have to trust Jarl. He'll find a way out. I want him rescued as much as you do, Saga. His parents are too powerful, and they will have guarded against you coming to get him."

Orlinza was right. Saga had already tried transporting to him once, even though she knew it was a bad idea. It was as if there were an impenetrable wall between Jarl and herself. She might have been able to find a way to sneak through it, but she wouldn't have been able to get back out.

Lashing her tail and pinning her ears, Saga paced through the clearing. She wanted to kick something, or fight someone, or do something to take her mind off her inability to rescue her friend.

Saga!

Jarl? She put her head up, looking around frantically for Jarl. She could sense him now and dashed off, leaving Orlinza behind. She would apologize later.

Jarl stood in the clearing where they usually entered and exited the *Through*. He smiled when he saw her and ran over, throwing his arms around her.

She leaned against him, almost knocking him over. *How did you get away?*

"Conor let me go." His expression fell into the sadness she was becoming used to. "He did have a good point, however. They're going to keep looking for me. I feel like we should make our base somewhere else. Maybe take a small group of people to train."

Aderyn rode up on Dega. "You made it out."

"Kind of," Jarl said. "Look, I don't think I should stay here. I was just telling Saga that we should find a separate base."

"We have been considering that. Perhaps it is time."

"Well, this is quaint. Where do you sleep? A cave?"

Jarl froze before slowly turning. Saga pinned her ears, too shocked to do anything else as Nessa, Jarl's mother, and a Farer she thought was named Tomal appeared. Both were dressed in full formal robes, and it would be clear to anyone watching that they were Vanaheim mages.

Jarl backed up until he bumped into her shoulder.

Saga, tell everyone to get off, now.

Saga passed his warning on to those near, and they would do the same. Except for the silent communication, everyone in the clearing simply stared. No one knew what to do.

Saga, get them out of here. Now!

Jarl's voice jolted her. He was terrified.

Everyone, go now! she ordered.

Nessa continued her quick assessment before her gaze fell on Brigid and Dance. Brigid whimpered.

112

That seemed to clue everyone else in the immediate area into the extreme danger they were all in.

"This is all your fault." Nessa pointed at Brigid.

Jarl threw out his hands, shouting as the bolt of killing energy fractured on a shield he threw between Nessa and her intended target.

"Go!"

Brigid didn't need any further encouragement. She swung up on Dance and they vanished.

Others did the same.

Aderyn and Dega galloped toward Nessa, sword raised.

"No! Just go!" Jarl yelled out. It was too late.

Nessa blasted them with the same bolt of energy, but Jarl's shield didn't hold up this time, and Aderyn was thrown from Dega's back. She crumpled to the ground, not moving.

Nessa threw another spell, and Dega's legs collapsed as she tumbled to the ground. Dead. Both were dead.

Saga screamed a challenge, and Jarl swung up on her bare back, legs clamped tight to her sides.

Nessa raised her eyebrows as if surprised Jarl would charge her.

Tomal stepped forward to engage Jarl while Nessa chanted, hands in the air.

We have to stop her, Jarl said.

Saga didn't answer, simply concentrated on keeping Jarl on her back as she dodged blasts from Tomal.

Jarl was very skilled at magical combat, but he didn't have near the power he used too, and was hard pressed to keep up with Tomal. He managed through

113

sheer determination. She could sense his energy lagging and knew they needed to end it quickly.

Jarl, shield me, and hang on.

She slammed into Tomal, trampling him. She shuddered as his skull and bones squished beneath her hooves. She would never get used to that feeling.

Jarl launched himself off her back, tackling his mother to the ground just as she released her spell.

They vanished.

Saga backed away as the magical energy spread skyward. At first nothing seemed to happen, then clouds rushed in from all directions, as if called to the spell. Blue lightning crackled upward and outward as the skies darkened. The clouds seemed to reach a critical point, now dark and heavy with water and sparkling with energy. They sped outward as quickly as they had come together, and Saga had no doubt that they would soon cover the entire world.

Rain started to fall.

Those who remained began to scream.

Saga stared for a moment, not quite sure what was going on, then she saw that wherever a drop fell, life simply stopped. Humans and Alfar fell in their tracks, grasses wilted, trees blackened.

No deadly rain fell where she stood, but that would change, she was certain.

Orlinza!

There was no reply. The Alfar was either dead or already gone. There was nothing she could do for the others as the drops of rain changed to a torrent that would soon overtake her.

Heart shattering, she fled the beloved home world she had only known for a short time.

She had to find Jarl. She couldn't lose him, too.

"What did you do?" Jarl stared at his mother where she lay sprawled on the ground.

He had tackled her, and she hadn't yet tried to stand after he backed away. Her eyes sparked with blue energy and her normally tidy hair stood out as if she had been struck by lightning.

Slowly, though the madness didn't leave her eyes, she smiled.

"Now you can come home."

"What?" Jarl shouted. "What did you do!"

"There's nothing for you to go back for." She finally stood. It was obvious she had used all her reserves casting her spell.

Jarl shivered at the look in her eyes.

"There will be no life left on that world by now. I'm sure some escaped, but we'll capture them soon enough. You may as well come home, Jarl. Your little rebellion is over."

The lack of menace in her expression chilled Jarl the most. She truly believed she had done the right thing and was extremely pleased that he could now come home.

"Mother, you destroyed a world?" He could barely say the words.

"It's no matter. I just wanted you to come home. Everyone will be so happy to see you." Her smile sickened him, and not just because of what she had done. She had lost her grasp on reality. Nessa had always been the most grounded mage he had ever known. Even more so than his father. Now she seemed vacant.

"Mother, how did you find me?"

115

"Oh, Conor, he put a tracking spell on you. It was an excellent plan." Her smile widened.

Jarl clenched his hands, betrayal twisting his gut and making him want to vomit. How could Conor? Had he known what Nessa intended?

"Now, take me home. It's time we got back to things."

What things they were supposed to get back to, Jarl didn't want to know. It occurred to him that if he wanted to kill his mother, now was the time. She was drained and probably wouldn't be able to put up much defense. Could he do it?

No.

He might regret it later, but for now she would live.

"Mother, you're going to have to wait until someone comes for you. I can't go back to Vanaheim. Ever." He might not be able to return to the Travelers after this either. He kept that to himself.

He looked around. He had taken them to one of the worlds the Vanier held. One that he and the Travelers hadn't managed to hit yet to destroy the Crystal.

"There is a small village that way." He pointed. "They'll help until Father comes to get you."

He suspected his father wouldn't have much trouble finding his mother. They always seemed to know where the other was. Some sort of magical binding or spell probably.

"You're not coming with me?"

"No! Not now, not ever! The Crystal is evil. It's destroying us. It's destroyed you."

Her happy expression fell. "Jarl, the Travelers are gone. You can come home. Conor won't mind giving

116

up the throne. I'm sure. And I know Ceridwen misses you."

Jarl's heart clenched as he backed away. "Go that way, Mother. I'm leaving now." He didn't know what else to do. Something told him he would regret not ending Nessa now, but what else could she do? She had already destroyed the Travelers' home world. Jarl was certain Saga still lived. He was also certain many had died. There were so many people on that world that wouldn't have had immediate access to a Traveler to escape. So many innocent lives.

Tears glistened in Nessa's eyes, only enhancing the madness he saw. Nessa never cried, never let emotion rule her. Now she had broken—and was perhaps that much more dangerous because of it.

"If you won't come home..."

Jarl didn't wait around to find out what she was going to say. His last view of his mother was of her raising her hands to cast another spell. Jarl let his powers take him, though he didn't have a clearly defined idea of where he was going to go.

It was dangerous to use his powers without a destination in mind, but he simply didn't know where to go.

He ended up in a familiar-looking clearing. The world with the pies, or so Saga claimed. What was it about pies?

He wasn't ready to go try to find the others, but he couldn't just sit around, so he headed down the dirt road, exhaustion more complete than he had ever felt, body and soul. His feet dragged across the dusty track and his shoulders drooped. What would he find?

Chapter 16

Saga found Jarl a few hours later. He sat on a bench across from the pie shop, staring at a pastry someone had probably given him. He didn't look up as she approached, just held out the hand tart. "Want this?"

Jarl, what happened? Are you okay?

She wasn't hungry, but she carefully lipped up the pastry, chewing as she studied her friend.

"Conor put a tracking spell on me. It's gone now, but I led them to your world. It's all my fault."

Saga pinned her ears, then nuzzled Jarl, smearing crumbs all over his arm. He didn't react.

It's not your fault, Jarl. You didn't expect Conor to betray you. You couldn't have known your mother would...do what she did.

"How bad is it?" Jarl still hadn't looked up.

Bad. She didn't have the heart to elaborate. Maybe she didn't need to. It was possible Nessa had told him what she had done.

"Do you know how many got away?"

Clearly, he knew. *No. We'll be regrouping for a while. I know where the majority of those who actually fight will have gone.*

Jarl sighed.

We should go.

For the first time, Jarl looked up. He seemed to have trouble focusing on her for a minute before he managed, completely exhausted. "Do you really think they want to see me? I just caused their entire world to be destroyed."

It wasn't your fault. Someday Jarl would believe her. She knew it to be true, even if she understood why Jarl felt the way he did.

"They're not going to be happy with me. Just, don't try to defend me when we get back."

Of course, I will defend you.

"I meant physically."

What do you mean?

"I'm sure at least one person is going to punch me in the face." Jarl half smiled at that before he stood on the bench and gestured for her to come up next to him.

He must be exhausted if he wasn't swinging up from the ground. Saga knew how he felt. She wished she could go directly to the world of dragons, where the others would be waiting. The danger was still too great.

You're sure they can't follow you anymore?

"As sure as I can be."

Then I am sure. I must leave town before we Travel. It won't take long after that.

"Okay."

Jarl's voice was empty, defeated. Surely the others wouldn't be as angry as Jarl thought they would be. She wasn't feeling very hopeful either.

∞ ∞ ∞

Jarl recognized the world Saga brought him to. It was the world where the dragons had lived. Another world destroyed by his people. Or at least another people. The world itself seemed okay because the dragons had sacrificed themselves to save it.

120

They rode for a while, and Jarl wondered if they would be able to recover Saga's saddle. He didn't mind riding bareback, but some things were easier with it.

Saga climbed the trail up to the dragons' plateau and stopped. Jarl heard voices and smelled a couple of campfires, though they were still hidden from view. He slid off of Saga, legs almost giving out, and he had to clutch her mane to keep from falling to the ground.

Jarl?

Just exhausted.

She nuzzled him and he patted her shoulder.

"So, you came back."

Jarl recognized William's voice, though it was a moment before the man stepped around a boulder, knife drawn.

Jarl held his hands out to the side in a placating gesture but didn't speak. What could someone say in a situation like this?

"I'm surprised you're not trying to plead your innocence," William snarled. He came over, snatched Jarl's arm, twisting it painfully behind his back.

Jarl winced but didn't resist, though he tried to flinch away from the knife now at his throat. William held him tight.

Saga snorted, stamping her foot. William ignored her.

"It is my fault. I didn't do it on purpose, but they did follow me."

The sharp edge of the knife pressed harder into his skin, drawing warm blood that dribbled down his neck.

Jarl's heart quickened, and he prepared a spell that would protect him if William decided to push any harder.

121

Saga snorted again, ears pinned. Jarl held eye contact with her, and she didn't approach. There wasn't much she could do unless he broke away, anyway.

"William, stop."

Jarl glanced over at Orlinza and sighed in relief. She was alive, at least.

"He as good as killed everyone, Orlinza."

"William, it wasn't his fault. We've been expecting an attack for a long time. It would have happened with or without Jarl."

"They didn't know where we were!" William hissed.

"They would have captured one of us, and they would have found out. It's done. We need to regroup, and killing Jarl won't help anything."

"It'll keep him from betraying us again."

"Jarl, please free yourself from William," Orlinza said.

Jarl frowned.

"Now." This time it was an order.

Smiling slightly, he whispered the last word of the spell and William froze, though he cursed.

Jarl, in control of William's body, pushed his arm away, and stepped over to Orlinza's side before releasing the angry man.

"Do you really think you would have succeeded? You didn't catch him off guard."

Jarl rubbed at his neck, surprised at how much blood William had drawn.

William glared. The man would never trust him again. Of course, Jarl was pretty sure he would never trust William either.

Saga stomped her foot again. *This is senseless.*

"Yes. We need to talk to the others, however tonight is not the night for plans, Saga. We need to rest and regroup. Tomorrow is soon enough to plot our next steps." Orlinza gestured for William to go ahead and he grudgingly obeyed.

While they walked, Orlinza briefly told him what had happened after he transported Nessa away.

"If only I had been a little faster."

She gripped his shoulder but didn't say anything. Jarl guessed she wished he had been a little faster, too.

The survivors were huddled around a fire near Tala's body. Jarl didn't sense the dragon, but he guessed the creature's spirit was around.

"Look who's showing his face," William growled as he stalked toward the fire.

The others, so few, looked up.

"You're alive!" Ima sprang up and threw her arms around Jarl. He managed to comprehend that she wasn't attacking him in time to not cast a spell on her.

Brigid, Ari, and only a handful of others also looked relieved. The Travelers nickered from where they stood a little farther back, grazing in a grassy patch.

"Am I the only one who isn't happy to see him?" William muttered.

"At the very least, he's the only powerful mage we have, William," Ima said. "We need everyone we can get if we're going to survive this."

Jarl cast about for Aderyn and Dega before remembering his mother had killed them. Their loss cut deep. He squeezed his eyes shut and fought tears.

"Is this everyone?" he asked as Ima pulled him to a spot around the fire.

"No. We had already taken many of the Alfar to another world for healing, and many of our people would have gone there. We lost many from our main camp. Others had more time to get away. Once we have some time to rest, we will meet up with everyone else," Ima said.

Rest sounded amazing to Jarl right then.

"You're injured? What happened?" Ima took a cloth from her pocket and dabbed at Jarl's neck.

"Just a scratch. I landed pretty hard when I transported Nessa off your world."

Jarl caught William glowering at him, but he didn't correct Jarl's story.

"Did you kill the other mage at least?" William asked.

Sighing, Jarl shook his head. "No."

William rocked back and threw his hands in the air. "You really are useless."

"If you say so," Jarl replied and leaned his elbows on his knees once Ima stopped dabbing at his neck.

"I think the bleeding has stopped, but you might end up with a scar if we can't get this cleaned up. We don't have any supplies. Most of us don't even have our tack."

"Everyone, let's rest," Orlinza stood. "I will see about preparing a meal. I want the rest of you to sleep."

Jarl stood to help her, and she leveled a finger at him. "You are in no condition to do anything but lay down and sleep."

He couldn't help but slide his eyes toward William, though Orlinza was probably the only one who noticed.

I will watch over you, Saga said apparently catching his thoughts.

Jarl nodded, though he wasn't sure if he would be able to sleep on the hard ground with the sun still high in the sky.

He barely made it over to a softer grassy spot before his eyes closed of their own accord and he collapsed to the ground.

Chapter 17

Though no one reacted as strongly as William had, reactions to Jarl's continued presence among them was as varied as he had feared. Saga wished she could fix it, but there was little she could do at the moment.

Because the Travelers generally preferred to be outside, they had not developed their home world much. The world they had chosen to stage the next part of their war from had many more buildings. They were currently in a large, open barn. Rain poured down outside, making everyone uneasy from recent memories, but it was warm and dry, and the owners had brought several long tables inside for the humans and Alfar to use while the Travelers stood.

Dega and Aderyn had been as close to a formal leader as the Travelers and their partners had. With them gone, no one was quite sure what to do, and no one was willing to step up and take over.

Finally, Orlinza stood from her place near one of the ends.

"This is ridiculous. Yes, Jarl is staying. No, he didn't bring the Vanir. Yes, we are going to continue to fight. We have no choice. The Crystal must be destroyed."

"How?" one of the Alfar shouted.

"A little bit at a time if we must," Orlinza said.

Jarl stood. "I've been led to believe, and not by the Vanir," he said, smiling slightly, "that if we can find the true main crystal cluster, we might be able to destroy it once and for all. Or at least severely weaken it enough that we will have a chance of taking out the other growths. The Vanir always thought the main growth was on Vanaheim. I don't actually think that is true. While I was…" He hesitated as if trying to choose what words to use. Saga could sense his confusion as to how to refer to his former home. Finally, he shrugged. "When I was last on Vanaheim, I had a fair bit of time to spend in the library, and I was able to do some research. I didn't find much unfortunately. My research does lead me to believe that if we can find the Dvergr, they might know."

"Great, so we're supposed to do that along with fight a war?" one of them said.

This is the key to winning the war, Saga said.

"How will we destroy the main Crystal even if we find it? It's hard to make enough of the dust to take out the smaller clusters," another said.

"Maybe we need a different method of destroying the Crystals," Jarl replied. "Maybe there's some kind of magic that will do it. I will think on it." He sat back down while the others thought about what he said.

"If it is possible to completely destroy it, we should do that," an Alfar Saga didn't know said. "That will be your task, Jarl. You are probably the only one with enough magical training to accomplish it."

Her partner nodded.

"The rest of us must decide how we can fight back with our diminished numbers. The Travelers lost many of their young. Many of the Alfar we rescued are too weak to fight, if they even survived the attack. Our Hauflin helpers were decimated. None of our supplies on the home world are accessible as the deadly rain continues to fall," the Alfar continued.

128

We must recruit more to our cause, Dance said. *Both Saga and I found partners amongst our enemy. There are many worlds out there and we may be able to find others as well.*

The Travelers generally agreed.

It will take us time to rebuild, but we will, Dance continued. *Not only must we fight back, but we must preserve what we are fighting for.*

Saga thought that mindset was wise but also hoped that they remembered that if they didn't fight, there would be nothing left to preserve.

As the meeting adjourned, Travelers and their partners and the rest moved into smaller groups, and a few went outside as the rain had subsided.

Jarl joined Saga. "I don't see any reason to wait. We should begin our search."

Saga bobbed her head.

Orlinza and Ima came over to them. "When will you leave?" Orlinza asked.

"Now."

"Be careful, Jarl. We still need you. Probably more now than ever." Orlinza hugged him.

"I will check in as frequently as I can. You are remaining on this world?"

"For now. I will make sure you can find me." She smiled.

"Rainer and I are going with you," Ima said.

Jarl glanced at Saga. *You can continue her training, and having another pair along will not be a bad thing.*

"Okay. We're leaving now."

"We're ready. Where are we going first?" Ima followed Jarl, and Saga gave Orlinza one last hug and then headed for the door.

"To get a new saddle and some weapons and supplies. And then we're going to find the Dvergr."

Saga flicked her ears forward in agreement.

"Okay. I need gear as well." She frowned.

"Then resupply will be our first mission. We need to find a place with a good saddle maker who won't ask questions and can work fast. We also need to find a way to pay."

"Magic?" Ima asked.

The first real smile Saga had seen in a while crossed Jarl's features. "Yes."

Chapter 18

Jarl stared out over the valley below them and contemplated their next move. Getting tack and weapons. Rainer knew of a world they could try. A place called Rim. It was his former partner, Tomas's home world. At one point there had been a talented saddle maker, and Rainer hoped he was still there, or had taught successors.

First, they had snuck onto a remote Vanir world that Jarl knew had significant deposits of gold. He had never been there, but Saga could use his knowledge to find it. They spent a tense afternoon watching a bunch of humans toil at a mineshaft before sneaking in after dark and stealing a bunch of the ore. Then they went back to the world where the dragons had once lived. The others had already vacated the plateau, so it was just the two Travelers, Ima and Jarl and the stony remains of the dragons to appreciate the breathtaking views and thin air.

"I would feel bad about stealing," Ima said. "If they hadn't just trashed the home world."

Jarl nodded, trying not to let the pain and guilt he felt show on his face as he worked on creating small ingots of gold they could trade for supplies and saddles.

"We will have to be careful not to buy all our supplies in one spot," Jarl said trying to change the subject. "We will attract too much attention otherwise."

"I will follow your lead. I have little experience with this sort of thing," Ima said.

"Where do you come from?" Jarl finished another ingot and very briefly wished for the extra power his rings had lent him. He would have been done an hour ago. Still, they had quite the stack of gold pieces and they would soon be able to head to Rim to try to get supplies and tack.

"I'm from Vanaheim. I escaped many years before you were born. I've been with the Travelers since."

Jarl wasn't sure how to respond, so he focused on finishing the last gold piece before replying. "I'm glad you were able to get away."

"Me, too."

They fell silent while Jarl collected the gold into a pouch. He left a few out. "Here, put these somewhere safe. As soon as we get more supplies, I'll split the rest with you in case we get separated."

"Thanks."

"In general, make sure you are someplace safe before you start showing that much gold. I'll see if we can get some of it broken into smaller currency once we're on Rim. Gold is pretty universal, however."

"I will watch and learn."

Jarl laughed. "You know, I'm not all that experienced with handling money either. It's not like I had much need at home."

"You have a valid point. At least we can defend ourselves if someone tries to take it."

Jarl nodded, sobering. "Let's go."

∞ ∞ ∞

The part of Rim that Saga and Rainer brought them to was a fairly standard agricultural village with fields of grains, pastures full of animals, and tidy houses with clay tile for roofing material. Until you looked up.

"What is that?" Ima asked.

"A moon?" Jarl stared.

Something moonlike took up a large portion of the sky, and it appeared to have to have rings around it. The sun, yellow like the one over Vanaheim, was high in the sky and it was probably midday, though instead of vibrant blue, the sky was purple and the moon with the rings had a lot of reds and yellows. It was beautiful and a little disturbing.

It's a planet, Saga said after a moment. *Rim is actually the moon.*

Jarl didn't even want to think about what that meant, so he just patted Saga's shoulder and urged her toward the town.

Rainer's memory proved accurate, and they found the saddle maker in a shop right off the town square. A livery and blacksmith stood next to it.

It seemed to be market day. Farmers and merchants lined the square with wagons of wares and people hurried about buying and selling goods. The smell of fresh food made Jarl's stomach rumble and the shouts and sounds of a happy populace made Jarl feel homesick for a moment.

They attracted a bit of attention as they rode into town. Bareback might have been ignored. Jarl hadn't thought about their lack of bridles. He should have cast a glamor. Cursing his lack of forethought, he slid off Saga's back when she stood by the hitching rail in front of the saddle maker's shop.

"Shards," he muttered.

133

"We get so used to not worrying about tack that we forget normal people use it any time they get on a horse." Ima sighed. "Oh well."

"Oh well is right. Let's hope they forget soon enough, or there truly aren't any connections to the Vanir here."

They both spoke in low tones to avoid anyone overhearing, though so far no one had come up to them.

Rainer nickered encouragingly.

"Well, let's see how badly this goes," Jarl said as he headed for the shop, Ima right behind him.

An older gentleman stood just inside the window and watched as they approached. He moved toward the door as Jarl stepped onto the creaky wooden step to the porch.

He opened it and gestured for Jarl and Ima to enter. Short, curly steel gray hair framed a dark-skinned face weathered by years in the sun. Wrinkles at his temples made Jarl think the man usually had a smile on his face, though he nearly frowned when he studied Jarl and Ima. He wore sturdy dark brown pants and a linen shirt.

The shop itself smelled of leather and saddle soap. Several work benches had pieces of harness or other tack in progress, and one table, with a soft-covered top had a nearly completed leather harness that looked fit for royalty.

"Hello," Jarl finally said. "I'm Jarl, and this is Ima."

The man's eyebrows rose, and he glanced out of the window again, possibly at the horses.

He seems suspicious, Saga said.

"We, uh, need saddles and bridles." Jarl tried to summon some of his normal confidence. It eluded him.

"I can see that," the man finally said. "What happened to yours? Clearly you can afford tack."

Jarl glanced down at his clothes when the man gestured at him. He wore his own clothing from Vanaheim. He had been wearing it for a couple of days and it didn't look that fine, to him. Apparently, this man thought otherwise.

He glanced at Ima, who shrugged.

"Fire," Jarl finally said.

"Don't you have your own saddle makers to tend to you?" The man turned his back on Jarl and Ima and went out to look at the Travelers.

"Maybe you should change your name, Jarl. And ditch the fancy clothing," Ima whispered. She didn't sound upset, just a little confused.

"Or at least I should have disguised us. Shards," he muttered.

"There is a fair bit of blue in your outfit."

Jarl sighed. "Maybe we should go somewhere else. They're not supposed to know anything on Rim, so Rainer thought."

"He still thinks they shouldn't know anything, but clearly something has upset this man."

He and Ima headed outside and Jarl twitched his fingers, wishing he still had his sword.

The saddle maker ran his hands over Saga's legs and back. She watched him, curiously. He patted her shoulder, murmuring a few quiet words that Jarl couldn't hear, then he studied Rainer.

"Where did you get this...?" He hesitated a moment longer, stroking Saga's neck. "Horse?"

"Shards," Jarl muttered again. "He knows something."

"Clearly," Ima whispered back.

"What business is it of yours?" Jarl finally managed to remember how to sound like a confident lord, and not a criminal.

"That's more what I would expect from your sort," the saddle maker said before turning back to Rainer. "I never forget a horse, though it's been years since I've seen this one."

Rainer snorted and shook his head.

Jarl, maybe we should go, Saga said uncertainly. *He is very concerned about us, and he does not like you.*

Maybe. Jarl decided to take a chance. Though there were a lot of people around, he and Ima could be mounted and gone before anyone could get close enough to help the saddle maker.

"You knew Tomas?" Jarl said.

The saddle maker straightened and looked at Jarl, hand still resting on Rainer's shoulder.

"Yes. Good lad, grew up near here."

Rainer shook his head, looking at Jarl.

What are you doing? Saga asked.

"I think it's okay, Saga," Jarl said aloud. "Tomas was killed not long ago. Rainer chose Ima as his partner. Saga has been with me since she was a foal."

The man studied Jarl before glancing at Ima again. "Let's say I believe you. What's one such as you doing with these folks?"

"One such as me?" Jarl really didn't want to go into it if he didn't have to, so he needed to know what the man suspected.

"Jarl is a Vanir name, and you're dressed like one of their mages."

"Ah," Jarl said. *So he does know more than is probably safe for him.*

I think he's worried that we are your prisoners.

"Well, if I had a choice, I would have gone to the man who originally made Saga's saddle, but since I have no wish to be killed by my own people, I'll stay off Vanaheim. I am one of their mages. Saga is my partner and since the Vanir are trying to enslave the Travelers, I'm trying to help stop it. Our tack was lost in a fight and we need to resupply."

They were starting to attract some attention from the marketgoers, and Jarl shifted uneasily.

"If you don't want our money, we'll go somewhere else." He put his hand on Saga's mane, ready to mount.

Rainer shifted uneasily and Saga perked her ears as she looked around for any additional danger.

"I'm pretty sure I don't believe you," the man said.

"I can tell. We'll leave," Jarl said.

"What if they don't want to leave?"

Jarl glanced up at the moon—planet—or whatever it was hanging low in the sky, looking for inspiration before he shrugged. "Then I'll leave on my own. I'm pretty sure you would be in for more of a fight than you could handle if you tried to detain Saga, and Rainer and Ima volunteered for the mission we're on."

"Sir," Ima spoke up. "I'm sorry you aren't happy with us, and we'll go somewhere else, but we really don't want to get into a fight with you. We will, if we have to. I'm also a mage, and it would go badly for you."

The man tilted his head and studied Ima for a moment. "Can you prove it?"

"What, that I'm a mage? I can zap you with lightning if you would like," she said shortly, obviously also annoyed.

"Hmm. Tomas was very clear about some things, including how Vanir treat Travelers and Alfar. Doesn't seem to be holding up."

"I'm sure whatever Tomas told you was quite correct. I'm not on their side, however." Jarl grabbed Saga's mane and swung his leg over her back. "We'll be going. We don't have a lot of time."

Saga laid her ears back, obviously glaring at the saddle maker before she turned on her haunches and made it clear she was only waiting for Rainer before she left.

"Well, if that's the case maybe we can talk. I'm Samal."

"Word of advice," Jarl said as he slid back off Saga. "If you ever do meet a more normal Vanir. Don't act like you know anything. If you're lucky, they'll just kill you if they find out you know more." He gestured for Samal to lead them back into the shop.

Chapter 19

He seems rather nice now, Saga said once they had a chance to actually talk with Samal. He accepted Jarl and Ima's story after a few more questions, and they fell to the question of tack. It would take longer than Jarl and Ima really wanted to wait for custom saddles. Samal had a few already made that he could fit to the Travelers. Bridles wouldn't take long, and he agreed to make the custom saddles anyway so they could come back for them. Jarl agreed to pay in advance. Samal had also exchanged some of their gold for local currency, and Jarl and Ima were now trying to get other supplies.

Yes, Jarl replied as he wandered around the general store.

While Jarl knew how to pack for an extended ride, Ima knew how to pack for an actual campaign. Some of what they needed this store didn't specifically have, such as bedrolls. She was able to gather bits and pieces that she assured Jarl would kit them out properly.

She finally stopped piling things on the counter and Jarl went over to pay. He could tell the woman behind the counter wanted to ask questions. Jarl just shrugged and paid when she told him the amount.

They gathered everything up and lugged it back to Samal's shop.

"Jarl, go get us some food while I put our kits together and make sure I'm not missing anything important," Ima said.

"Anything in particular I should look for?"

"Food that will travel well, and maybe something for lunch."

Jarl caught Samal watching the exchange but didn't let on that he noticed. "I'll be back shortly."

"Thanks, Jarl."

"Of course, Ima."

He hesitated to leave them alone, but she could take care of herself, and Saga could shout if there was trouble. He might be in more danger out in the market.

No longer attracting attention due to the glamor he had cast on his clothing earlier, Jarl moved through the crowd and listened to the chatter. So many worlds spoke close variations of the Vanir language, and it wasn't hard to be understood here. Accents varied, but the words were similar. There were many places that wasn't the case, and generally magic provided the answer for mages. He wasn't sure what the Travelers and their partners did if they didn't know the local dialect. Another thing he would have to find out eventually.

Jarl found a few stalls with likely travel rations, stocked up, and then selected something for lunch, buying enough for Samal. As he was headed back to the shop, another store caught his eye. Rugged clothing, well-cut and made for the outdoors. He almost went inside the shop, but his arms were full.

Making a note of the place, he planned to return before they left the world.

He had originally thought they shouldn't resupply all in one location. He had finally decided they should just get it over with instead of risking another screw up on a different world. This one hadn't gone as poorly as it could have, but he had no desire to make new mistakes. At least for supplies. Not knowing anything about the Dvergr he was quite certain he would make some there. Hopefully not fatal ones. If they could even find the elusive beings. Saga had an idea of where to start.

Samal paused in his saddle fitting to eat with them when Jarl returned with food. They didn't talk much, not knowing what to say. Though Samal had asked about news, Jarl had suggested it was safer if he didn't know anything and Ima had agreed.

"I'll have those saddles adjusted before long. Saga asked for some extra straps to make them secure should you have to fight. Ima explained that Saga is an accomplished combatant herself and she's not happy with the way the saddle might slide since it's not custom made for your purpose. If you do make it back, the new one will suit you better."

"Thank you," Jarl replied, finishing lunch. "Do you mind if I steal Ima away for a few minutes."

"No. If Saga or Rainer have anything else they need me to adjust, I will work it out with them, or ask when you return." Samal wiped off his hands and went back to the bridles. "I'm almost finished with their bridles. I was able to make some removable bit straps in case you need to disguise them."

"Again, thank you."

Samal nodded and bent to his work.

Ima and Jarl left the shop.

"What did you want?" Ima asked.

"Thought it might be nice to have a change of clothing, or two." Jarl tugged at his sleeve. "It's a nice shirt, but I kind of want to get rid of it."

"Keep it for now, Jarl. You may need it later." Ima shrugged. "Some clothing would be good, and I think we will have room in our supplies. I forget we have plenty of money. That's not always the case."

Jarl smiled. "We know where to get more if we need it."

She laughed.

∞ ∞ ∞

Provisioned and with reasonably comfortable tack considering the short notice—the Travelers had no complaints; the riders had to get used to the new saddles though—they set out that evening.

Neither Jarl nor Ima wanted to spend the night someplace they had just spent so much money, so she suggested another world she knew where they could rest and plan to hunt for the Dvergr.

Of course, when they arrived, it was the middle of the day.

Ima laughed. "I'm sorry. Sometimes this happens. We should still rest. Everyone is exhausted."

Jarl still hadn't recovered from the mental fatigue of fighting his mother, and Saga's steps dragged, as did Rainer's. Ima seemed to be in the best condition of all of them, and even her shoulders slumped.

"We need weapons next," Jarl said. "After we sleep."

I know of a place, Saga said. *Tomorrow. Weapons, and then we will go to the Dvergr and maybe they will tell us where to hunt the Crystal.*

"Let's hope we know when we've found it," Jarl said.

"I think we will." Ima shuddered.

142

Chapter 20

I have never been here, Saga said. *I think I remember a story about stone dwellers and this world, however.*

The trees that surrounded them had a reddish cast to the leaves and a silver glint to the bark. Jarl's lungs struggled in the thin air, but the cool crispness refreshed him after the hot humidity of the last world they had been on.

The cloaks they now wore had been cheap due to the season on the world where they had purchased them. The seller simply wanted them gone. The swords, a short one for Saga that Jarl still had to wrap in leather so she could grip it, a saber for him, and another short sword for Ima had cost them dearly. The daggers hadn't been as expensive, but if Jarl hadn't had a reasonably easy source of gold to exploit, he would have been worried about their funds.

As it was, they would have to steal more soon, if they stayed out long.

Jarl knew he had been overcharged, though the weapons were quality, and he didn't care. They just needed to be armed and gone.

This way, I think, Rainer added.

Saga followed him down the narrow game trail and Ima and Jarl ducked low to avoid branches from the leafy trees.

Jarl hoped that whatever innate sense the Travelers had that helped them navigate through the worlds, would help them now. No one had seen the elusive Dvergr in generations, but they had to be somewhere. They had to have existed. So many different races had stories of the stone workers.

He didn't know what he would do if they didn't find any clues.

They had to end this war.

Rainer led them for a while, then Saga took the lead when they broke out of the trees into a high rocky expanse. If Jarl would have had any breath the views would have taken it away. As it was an oily voice in the back of his mind distracted him.

He frowned and looked around. "Did anyone else hear that?"

"No?"

The Travelers both tossed their heads in a negative.

Jarl shook his head. He couldn't get rid of the faint whisper.

Soon the vegetation vanished completely, and the rock began to fracture under the Travelers' hooves.

"Seems like there's a certain parasite about," Ima said.

"That's what I'm hearing," Jarl grumbled.

"You are likely more in tune with it than the rest of us."

Jarl didn't answer, but she was right.

Soon spikes of the beautiful, yet deadly, blue Crystal stood out amongst the rocks. It pulsed faintly and some part of Jarl wanted to take up the Crystals and feel their power again. The rest of him shuddered in revulsion.

As they went farther, it became clear they followed an overgrown path. Rubble obscured quite a bit of it, though it caused little difficulty for the

Travelers. Before long the path led them away from the outcroppings of Crystal and down into a small valley. Here the faint path ended in a rock-strewn cave entrance.

If Jarl hadn't known he was looking at something made by people instead of nature, he wouldn't have noticed the remnants of the worked stone arch, or what looked like carvings in some of the stones.

He dismounted and Ima did the same.

"Saga, why don't you or Rainer go check in. We're going to have to go on foot and I don't think you will be able to make it," Jarl said.

Saga laid her ears back but bobbed her head. She and Rainer conferred briefly before he touched Ima gently with his nose and trotted away.

He would be able to come directly back to Saga's location now that they knew where to look.

Ima went up to the opening while Jarl spoke with Saga.

"This opening was originally made with tools. Or magic."

Jarl nodded his agreement. "Be ready to cast a shield spell." He readied the spell and the insistent whispers grew louder. They almost seemed triumphant. Shuddering, Jarl picked his way over the boulders as he followed Ima into the darkness.

She cast a illumination spell, making the rocks sparkle in the brilliant light. Some sort of natural mineral probably. Jarl didn't know much about rocks beyond magical properties.

They followed the rock-strewn passageway for close to an hour before it ended. A pair of wooden doors, rotten with age or the effects of the Crystal, blocked the way.

Jarl pulled on the handle and it came away in his hand. Ima arched her eyebrows before shrugging and pushing. The wood crumpled to the floor, and they picked their way carefully through the splintered remains before pausing on the other side. The air smelled old and stale, but fresh enough to breathe so they proceeded.

The blue glow from the Crystal almost made Ima's light irrelevant, the beautiful yet deadly parasite lighting the vast cavern. The uneven blue light showed Jarl what he had feared as soon as they knew the Crystal was present on this world. Nothing living was left. There must have been some sort of life or magic still present as the Crystal hadn't spread much beyond the cavern.

"Jarl!" Ima grabbed his hand and pulled him back.

Jarl jerked and looked around. He had taken several steps toward the nearest outcropping of Crystal without even realizing it.

Her hand trembled on his, and he didn't think it was from the effort of holding him back.

"Let's go." Her voice shook.

Jarl shuddered again and nodded. "There's nothing here but the parasite, and there's no way anything has survived."

"I'm not so sure about that, but it's trying really hard to take control of you. We need to get you out of here. If you lose your mind, I can't stop you." Ima's eyes were wide when they met Jarl's.

He swallowed and turned for the entrance just in time to see something swinging at his face.

∞ ∞ ∞

"Jarl!"

He groaned and tried to clutch at his aching skull. His hands wouldn't respond.

"Jarl, are you okay?"

It sounded like Ima's voice. He hoped that meant whoever had hit him hadn't been Vanir. Or they probably wouldn't have left his Alfar friend anywhere near him.

Jarl forced his eyes open, wincing as lights flashed in his vision and pain stabbed at him. "What happened?"

"You got hit in the face by a tree branch."

"I don't remember any trees in the cave," he grumbled. The air still felt cool, though less stale and as awareness returned, he could feel a blanket or something under him. The ground underneath was hard and cool. His hands were tied behind his back, and he lay on his side.

"It was only a branch," Ima said casually. "The tree had parted ways with it a while ago."

Jarl twisted around so that he could see her. She wasn't usually prone to humor and at least from Jarl's perspective it didn't seem like a good time to make fun of the situation.

"You've got some amazing bruises on your face." Ima sat across from him, leaning against a stone wall. Steady light illuminated the space and Jarl wondered if she or someone had lit mage lamps.

Ima wasn't tied, and she seemed happy for some reason.

Jarl briefly considered the possibility that Ima had betrayed him, but just couldn't believe it. Besides, Rainer and Saga would have known.

Saga!

He managed to get upright and on his knees before Ima held out a hand.

"Relax, Jarl. The Travelers are okay. Saga is quite upset, but they're fine."

"What's going on?"

Ima sighed. "We found, or perhaps the better phrase is, were found by, a group of Alfar and humans who have lived on this world for quite some time. They've been working to contain the Crystal and their mage was overcome. They want you to help save her."

Jarl blinked a few times, trying to process her words. "They want me to help them so they hit me in the face and tied me up?"

"Well, they thought the Crystal had taken control of you."

Jarl groaned again. "I think I'm just going to go back to being unconscious." He flopped back down to the ground as gently as he could manage with bound arms, though he kept watching Ima.

Saga?

All is well, Jarl. Are you okay?

Yes. He turned his focus back to Ima.

"Jarl, if we can help them, maybe they can help us. I already asked; they don't know where the Crystal comes from. Apparently their mage had developed a way to destroy the Crystal independent of the Travelers' method. It's not easy, but you should be able to do it. They tried to explain it to me. I just don't have the magical experience necessary."

"Why am I tied up then?"

Ima averted her eyes for a moment before shrugging. "They don't trust you."

Jarl rolled his eyes and sighed. "Yes, well, about the only one who does is Saga."

"I trust you."

Jarl arched an eyebrow.

148

"I do. They took my weapons though, and it will be easier to cut the ropes off than to untie them. They're tight. I already tried."

He took a deep breath and nodded, though his face still ached and shot pain through his neck and shoulders when he tried to move again. He felt guilty about his words but didn't think she was upset by them.

"So, what do we do next?" Jarl was tired of being the one to come up with answers. Perhaps Ima would have some.

"Next you convince us we should trust you," a new voice said. "Otherwise we will kill you."

Chapter 21

"Thought you wanted my help," Jarl said through gritted teeth, not bothering to look at his captor. He could still sense the oily presence of the Crystal, but it was faint enough that he was pretty sure he could use magic without it hindering him. He didn't need his hands to cast a spell. In fact...he concentrated on the ropes that bound him.

"We do. But a Vanir mage without his Crystal rings is still a Vanir and the enemy." The person who spoke had a masculine voice but Jarl wasn't sure if he was human or Alfar.

Jarl sighed. He was getting tired of that sentiment. Not that it wasn't deserved, but he was still annoyed.

"He's on our side," Ima said, voice sharp.

The ropes disintegrated and Jarl sat up, bringing his hands in front of him and shaking them out. He finally looked at the person who had entered the room. An older human with short graying hair and a gray beard stared at Jarl. He wore heavy canvas pants and a wool sweater and wouldn't have been out of place on a fishing vessel. Though as far as Jarl knew they were far from any large body of water.

The man took a step back when it was clear Jarl had freed himself. He didn't sound the alarm, just crossed his arms and glared.

"I'm Jarl. You've met Ima I believe." Ignoring the lingering ache in his skull, Jarl stood.

The other man regarded Jarl for a moment before shrugging. "Graesin. Come with me."

Jarl shared a glance with Ima before they followed.

Graesin led them out of the room they had been in, and into a darker corridor. The walls were worked stone and Jarl still had the feeling they were in a cave system. Probably the same one or Saga might have been more upset. He could sense her following his progress with their bond, but she wasn't interfering. Jarl wondered how Ima had managed to get Saga to stay where she was.

The bare stone hallway, lit by a steady strip of light that went across the ceiling and might have been a version of mage lighting, led them to a larger room. This one was round, lined with shelves and work benches, and had a body lying on a cot in the center. Jarl spared a quick glance for the shelves, noting that they were full of vials and containers and reminded him very much of some of his classrooms back at Mageheim.

The body drew most of his attention. She was a younger woman, perhaps a few years older than he was. Long red hair framed pale skin and freckles scattered across her nose. He wouldn't have been surprised if she had green eyes, but they were shut. She wore similar clothing to Graesin, and greens dominated the colors. A light blanket covered her, and she didn't move.

Graesin stepped to her side and pulled the blanket back.

Ima gasped and Jarl tensed. Like the dragons, the Crystal had taken over her lower legs, growing into her and apparently taking over her body.

"This is Una. She and Saira, were attacked by the Crystal while they attempted to destroy it. Saira was practiced at the method. Una was learning. Unfortunately, we lost Saira in the battle. If you can learn the method, will you save Una?"

Jarl stared at Una's legs and shivered. "Yes, but how will I learn it? If you had someone else, I'm sure you would already have tried. And how did the Crystal fight back?" That part disturbed Jarl. So far he had only encountered people controlled by the Crystal fighting him, not the creature itself.

"Somehow it overcame their minds and they fell unconscious. Before we could get to them it had grown over Saira completely, and into Una's legs. We've been fighting this infestation for years, and we've managed to push it back into the cave system and surrounding areas but haven't been able to eradicate it completely. It is strong."

Saga, do they have any dust available? We might be able to help them. At least for her legs.

I will find out.

Jarl crossed his arms and studied Una while Graesin watched.

"Can he help?" An Alfar with dark skin and light green hair entered the cavern. She was armed with a short sword and a scowl marred her features.

Jarl spared her a glance before returning his gaze to Una. He studied the growths spearing her legs. Even if they could kill the parasite, could they save her legs?

"He hasn't said," Graesin replied.

Jarl didn't bother to answer, the ache in his head a reminder that he wasn't among friends.

Ima also remained quiet, perhaps not knowing if they could help or not.

I've returned, Jarl. I have some of the dust. It's not much, but it should be enough to kill the Crystal in her legs. Will it hurt the human?

I really don't know. I'll come to you. There's not a lot of room here.

Jarl glanced at Ima and could see by her raised eyebrows and slight smile that Rainer had filled her in on at least part of the plan.

"I'm going to go get something from Saga. I'll return in a moment," Jarl said.

The Alfar woman leveled a sword at Jarl. "You'll not leave."

Jarl sighed, extremely tired of the uncalled-for treatment from these people. "You can't stop me."

Before they could react, he gripped Ima's arm and used his Farer ability to transport them from the caverns to Saga and Rainer.

Ima hugged her companion, and Jarl leaned against Saga. She wrapped him in the equine version of a hug, head pressed into his back.

"Thanks."

Of course, Jarl. The dust is in my saddlebags. The others are preparing to assault Vanaheim. They think it's the only way. They want you to return soon so we can talk of it.

"Okay. Ima, ready to return?"

She held out her hand. Jarl took it, though strictly speaking he didn't need to be touching her like the Travelers did. He brought them back into the cave.

Graesin, the other Alfar, and another human male were arguing with each other. They stopped when Jarl and Ima returned.

Jarl pretended like nothing had happened and knelt next to Una. "Okay, we're going to try to heal her while the Crystal is killed. I have no idea if this is going to work. We know she will die if the Crystal isn't dealt with."

"You know healing?"

Jarl shook his head. "I know some basics, but I'm not a healer. However, even the basics will be better than nothing. Ima will lend me strength."

He glanced at the other mage and she nodded agreement and understanding before kneeling next to him and putting her hand on his shoulder.

"This dust will destroy the Crystal." He held out the pouch and looked at Graesin and the other two. They gestured for him to continue after a quick shared glance.

Jarl sprinkled the powder on the Crystal growths and watched for a moment as they began to crack and ooze blue liquid.

Una's eyes snapped open and she gasped. Jarl suspected that was a reaction from the Crystal, not the woman herself. Before he could lose too much time, he let his magic pour into the woman and promote healing in her body. Ima lent her strength to Jarl.

His headache immediately worsened, and his legs ached as he took some of the pain from Una.

He wasn't sure how long he worked on the woman, lending her strength, trying to heal her body as the Crystal left it, before he blacked out. He came to on a much softer pallet. Despite the warm blanket that covered him, he shivered, each tremor sending splinters of pain through his temples.

"Ima," he gasped, wincing as even his whisper pierced his skull. *Saga?*

Ima is with the woman. I'm here. Are you okay?

Yes. Another tremor rattled his head. *No. But I will be okay. Do you know how the mage is?*

She's awake, but Rainer said she is confused.

155

Jarl groaned, regretted making any noise, and squeezed his eyes shut. He desperately wanted to go back to sleep, but he forced himself to push the blanket back and climb to his feet.

Maybe you should rest, Saga said.

Probably. Jarl staggered toward the doorway, digging the heel of his palm into forehead to try and alleviate some of the pressure.

Which way? He asked Saga after looking into the stone passage and seeing he had two choices.

To your right. Saga sounded resigned, as if she knew he wouldn't rest even though he needed it.

One hand on his head, one hand trailing on the cold stone wall of the cave system for balance, Jarl managed to make it a short distance down the corridor. He came to another side passage. This one was short and he could hear voices and see a lit room. It looked familiar so he headed toward it.

"Jarl!" Ima said when she saw him. "You shouldn't be up."

"I'm well aware," he said, wincing in the brighter light.

He is stubborn, Saga said, but she didn't sound mad.

Ima smiled in agreement.

Graesin and the Alfar woman from earlier were sitting next to Una. She sat in a chair with a blanket over her legs and stared back at them, eyes not quite focused.

Ima took Jarl's arm and supported him as he walked over to join them. "At least sit," she said as she pushed him into a third chair.

Jarl sank down gratefully and considered closing his eyes right there. He resisted.

"Una?"

She turned her head and looked at him, eyes glassy, almost as if she had a concussion. She had the look of a mage who had drawn too deeply of the Crystal's powers and was lost to them.

"We need to block her connection to the Crystal completely," Jarl said through gritted teeth. "The sooner we do it, the faster she will recover. I've heard of this sort of thing in mages who overdo their magic use."

"Like you?" Ima said sharply.

"No. I wasn't drawing on the Crystal's power, just my own and yours." He shut his eyes for a moment trying to regain some of his strength. "If I'd had the Crystal's power too, I wouldn't have passed out."

The others shifted uncomfortably, except for Una who just stared at him.

"I don't think she will recover without blocking her abilities," Jarl said. "I also don't know if it can be undone. She may not thank me if she does recover."

"Do it," Graesin said.

Jarl mustered the last of his reserves. Ima again lent him some of her power. He still had to resist reaching out to the nearby Crystal infestation to boost his strength. Clenching his jaw, Jarl put his hand on Una's arm. She didn't resist, simply watched with vacant eyes.

Quickly, he searched with his magic for any hint of the Crystal left in her body and didn't find any. He could sense that she still was connected to it, as he probably was, and that the Crystal seemed to be using her still, forcing her out of her own mind.

Jarl built a shield and infused it with wards that would cut her off from any magical abilities. It was difficult, and he had only performed the spell once before with the aid of all of his rings and a full night's

157

rest, but it was the only way he knew of to cut someone off from the Crystal without outright killing them and clearly it still had control of her.

Ima sent him more power when he wavered.

Before he could question his actions, before he could hesitate at cutting another mage off from their power, he thrust the warded shield into place.

He felt the presence shoved from Una's mind, felt its rage, and he managed to pull back into his own mind before it retaliated.

Jarl! Saga shouted as the Crystal struck through his own connection to the parasite.

He grabbed onto Saga's presence and used it to anchor his mind firmly and throw up his own shields. The effort cost him his last thread of consciousness.

Chapter 22

Jarl! Saga lashed her tail, rearing slightly in frustration.

Ima says he's unconscious, but not injured that she can see. She thinks he simply over did it helping Una, Rainer said.

The Crystal attacked him when he freed Una. Saga lashed her tail again. *I'm going to him.*

Saga traveled into the *Through* a short hop and came out in a small cave. While she was very used to being inside, having grown up in a castle, it had been a long time since she was in a confined space and she flattened her ears and ignored the gasp of surprise from a person who sat nearby.

Jarl lay on a cot with a couple of wool blankets pulled up to his chin. He breathed quietly and his expression seemed peaceful. She thought that meant he had pushed the Crystal away before he had lost consciousness. She thought he had from what she could sense but wasn't sure.

She nuzzled him and wished for one of her bowl couches. Jarl, still asleep, reached up and put his hand on her forehead. She blew out softly through her nostrils and took in his scent. Not that she was sure she would be able to smell anything different, but he smelled like himself. That was promising. She hoped.

"Saga?" he muttered, eyes still shut.

Yes.

He winced when she spoke to him.

Are you okay?

"Worst headache of my life." He groaned. "Worse than the time I blew up the lab."

Saga snorted her equivalent of laughter.

"Is he okay?"

Saga looked up from her friend and studied the woman who sat nearby.

"I'm fine. Basically," Jarl said though he didn't open his eyes. "How is Una?"

"She's…" the woman, an Alfar Saga saw, started, "She's alive. And she's herself again."

"But she's understandably upset at what I did," Jarl filled in the blank that the Alfar's hesitation left.

"Yes."

He sighed. "Well, no one else is happy with me either, so she can join the group."

Jarl.

It's true, Saga.

She nuzzled her friend again.

"She understands you saved her life. She is grateful."

Jarl slowly opened his eyes, wincing again. "I'm sure she is."

"How do you feel?" The Alfar woman came over to his side.

"About like you might expect."

She nodded. "My name is Nyra. I don't believe I had a chance to introduce myself earlier."

"Jarl," he replied though it was obvious Nyra knew who he was. "And this is Saga."

"Greetings. When you are feeling up to it, you should talk to Una."

160

"I can talk to her any time. Doing more magic is going to take some actual rest and maybe a meal or two."

"Of course. We thank you for saving her. I'll see about food. Do your companions need anything?" She glanced at Saga.

Oatcakes? Saga said perking her ears, though she felt that might be asking for too much.

Jarl relayed her request, and Nyra smiled. "It will take a little time, but I think we can manage something."

Thank you.

Nyra left the room.

Jarl, if Una can teach you to kill the Crystal with magic, then all we need to do is find the source and this war will be over.

Jarl sat up and patted Saga on the shoulder. "You are ever the optimist, my friend."

She flicked her ears forward before shaking her head.

He held his head for a moment. "There doesn't happen to be any water around here, does there?"

Saga glanced around. *Only what I carry.*

Jarl looked at Saga, eyes slightly unfocused. He frowned and seemed to concentrate on her. "Do you want me to untack you?" He stood and found his water skin, drinking while he leaned against her.

No, not just yet.

"Okay, let's go talk to Una."

Shouldn't you rest? Saga could feel how weary Jarl was through their bond, and the way he clutched at her tack.

"I'll have to soon, but I want to talk to Una, and I need to stay awake long enough to eat, so I may as well do something while we're waiting."

I do not think the doorway is big enough for both of us at once. Saga nickered gently.

"No. I'll go first. Catch me if I fall."

She nudged him, and then, feeling like a colt following a human eager for the grain they carried, followed close behind.

He made it to the next room over, though Saga was beginning to wish she had let him untack her. The walls were narrow enough as it was without the saddle adding to her width. She stuck her head in the doorway but remained in the hallway.

A woman who had to be Una sat in chair covered in blankets and sipped something from a steaming mug. Another man sat by her, who Saga thought was Graesin from Jarl's memories.

"Jarl, it appears you were able to save Una, thank you," Graesin said.

"You're welcome," he said absently, his attention on the young woman.

"Yes, I am grateful to have my mind back. Thank you." She smiled though her eyes didn't reflect the smile. She glanced over at Saga then back to Jarl. "Your companion is beautiful."

Saga nickered, pleased at the compliment.

"Her name is Saga, and she says thank you," Jarl replied.

"I know Graesin wants me to teach you how to destroy the Crystal, but I'm not sure if I can, now that I can't touch magic." She took one hand from her mug and put her fingers to her temple.

"Give me some time, and I will see if I can reverse that. We should wait until the Crystal is gone from this world. Tell me what you can, and I will see if I can work it out."

Saga watched while they fell into a discussion about the technical aspects of magic use and what they did to the Crystal.

Jarl seemed to follow and agreed to try it after they rested.

Someone cleared their throat behind Saga, and she startled backward.

Sorry, Saga said reflexively directing the thought at the woman, though she wasn't sure Nyra could hear her. Most Alfar could.

"Not a problem. I brought food. Where would you like me to set your oatcakes?"

Putting the plate on the ground is fine. I should save some for Rainer.

Coming!

Before Saga could advise the other Traveler of the tight conditions, he appeared in the hallway and snatched an oatcake.

She nickered laughter and joined him.

The Alfar's eyebrows rose as she smiled and took the rest of the food inside for Jarl.

Chapter 23

A solid night and half a day of sleep did wonders for Jarl's energy levels, and his mood. He almost felt like his old self for a few minutes when he woke up.

Saga?

I'm grazing with Rainer outside.

I'm ready to try the spell on the Crystal.

Eat first.

I will, and find Ima. She needs to learn, too. Saga didn't reply. He sensed that she agreed and was pleased, though she had turned her attention back to the soft mountain grasses.

Jarl grinned and left the small room he had slept in. For a minute he stood in the cave hallway and tried to get his bearings. The last couple of days he hadn't really paid much attention to his surroundings. The cave walls were reasonably uniform. Here and there veins of some sort of mineral ran through them, sparkling in the lamp lights. They kept the areas they lived in well lit, but the uneven lighting did lead to shadows and Jarl hoped this world didn't have anything the equivalent of the Ovatar shadow creatures from his world.

After a minute he turned right, trying to remember which direction he needed to go.

He passed a couple of rooms that were more alcoves than rooms. A couple of them looked natural. A few of the bigger ones had some sharp angles that made it look like they had been worked with tools. They obviously didn't have many mages, or it would have been much easier to do with magic. Of course, most mages he knew also wouldn't have wanted to lower themselves to something akin to manual labor.

After a moment he smelled food. Good. He chose the correct direction. Following his nose led him to a larger cavern filled with wooden tables lined with benches. These people must have lived here for quite some time. The benches were well crafted from wood and looked comfortable. A few humans and Alfar sat together near the back. The food smells came from that direction as well, and he headed over.

The others stopped talking and glanced at him when he approached. He ignored their stares, used to it by now, and pushed through the swinging doors into what turned out to be the kitchen.

The delicious smells intensified, and a plate of oatcakes sat on a platter near the door. Grinning, he sent a quick thought toward Saga, letting her know they had some ready.

"Jarl, correct?" An older, dark-skinned woman with a smile on her face came into view around a corner. She wore a long tan apron over a spun green-colored dress. Long, dark hair flowed down her back.

"Yes."

"I'm Toni. Graesin is my husband. Are you looking for food?"

Jarl couldn't help but return her smile. It seemed like forever since someone smiled that sincerely at him.

"Yes."

"Then you came to the right place."

"Thank you." It was such a relief to see an openly friendly face that Jarl's throat tightened, and he had to rub at his eyes for a moment.

Shortly, Toni returned carrying a tray laden with meat and cheese, as well as a glass.

"Is this okay?"

Jarl smiled. "Yes, thank you." He took the tray from her and went back out into the dining area. He was rather suddenly aware of how hungry he was, and the food was gone in moments, without him really tasting it. Though he did have the impression of smoky cheese and good-tasting meat.

He brought the tray back to the kitchen area, where a young, lighter-skinned man, took his tray.

Saga, would you mind asking Ima to meet me?

Of course, Jarl. She's coming.

Before long, Ima walked quickly down the carved-out tunnel toward him.

"Ready?" She grinned in anticipation.

"Yes."

"I've also been talking with Uma. I think I know what to do."

"Good. The last bit of the Crystal is strong." Jarl frowned, almost certain he could hear the parasite's oily whispers even now. "It will take a lot of effort."

"Are you okay?" Her smile faded. "We can wait if you need more rest."

"No, it's not that. It's more that I still think I can hear it. And that worries me."

"Me as well. You be sure to let me know if it gives you any troubles. I don't need to try to fight the Crystal through you." Ima shuddered.

Jarl took a deep breath. "I don't want that either."

Saga, keep watch please.

167

She would know exactly what he meant, and he sensed her agreement, and worry.

"Do you know the way to the caves?"

"Follow me."

They walked in silence for a while and Jarl contemplated the upcoming fight against the Crystal parasite. Would he be able to defeat it without drawing power from it? What would he do once he came up against his family in battle again? Trying not to worry about something that was, unfortunately, inevitable, he turned his mind away and tried to concentrate on the focusing exercises he had learned in his basic classes years and years ago.

It worked and he was as ready as he could be. Though he could feel the Crystal digging against the shields that armored his mind.

"Should we do it together?" Ima asked. "Since neither of us have done this before, it might be a good idea."

"If we join our powers together that closely, you would be in significant danger if the Crystal manages to attack my mind."

"Jarl, even with everything you've taught me, I can't stand against you. I'm in danger either way, and do you honestly think you can do this alone? Even I can feel how strong this outcropping of Crystal is."

Something in his expression must have answered Ima for him, because she held out her hands.

They had practiced sharing energies, and had even done it a time or two, but this would be the first time in a while that Jarl had needed another mage's help to perform a spell beyond healing Una. Everyone was taught how to link with another, but typically only the less powerful mages ever needed to do it.

He took a deep breath and took her warm hands in his. After a moment they both drew on their mage sight, and the magical energies drew into both of them and twined together.

He opened his mind to her and extended his shields to enclose her. Briefly, he thought about giving her the lead, then he thought about the danger that put her in and decided against it.

Together they shaped the spell in their mage sight, weaving threads of energy into the proper shaft of magic that would destroy the last of the malignant growth on this world.

It didn't take long for the Crystal to sense their intent, and it renewed its efforts against Jarl's mind. His mental armor held, and as long as the Crystal didn't find some sort of crack or weakness due to his long and close association with the parasite, they would be fine.

Ima met his eyes as they worked, her eyes bright with the energies that flowed through both of them.

Jarl half smiled back at her as she took a step forward. The distance between the two of them closed to almost nothing as they immersed themselves in the spell, weaving the final shapes with their hands still joined.

The Crystal shrieked, striking at Jarl's concentration when it couldn't penetrate his shields any other way.

He and Ima flinched. She held the spell shape while he reinforced their protections.

"We have to drop some of our protections to get the spell out," Jarl said. "We will have to move fast."

She nodded, brow furrowed, moisture gathering at her temples.

Jarl blinked sweat from his eyes, and they both turned to the Crystal, one of his hands still clasped in Ima's.

Taking a deep breath, Jarl dropped the protections that kept the spell energies contained.

The Crystal must have expected it, because it stabbed at Jarl as soon as the shields weakened.

He doubled over in pain, clutching his head with his free hand. Ima held the spell fast while Jarl dealt with the attack.

Ima cried out. "Jarl, hurry."

Using every spare scrap of energy, he pushed the assault back, dropping to a knee unable to keep his feet.

"Now!"

He and Ima pushed the wedge of magic at the Crystal with all their ability.

The Crystal screamed and sent daggers of magic flinging toward them.

Jarl leapt up and tackled Ima to the ground shielding her physically, as well as with magic as the Crystal's attack struck.

He cried out as shards lashed against him, digging into his skin. Through the hazy pain he felt the Crystal's presence evaporate away.

"Jarl, are you okay?" Ima said a short time later.

"Maybe." He wasn't actually sure. His entire body felt numb, though he did realize he was still sprawled across Ima, protecting her from a threat that no longer existed. "Sorry." He groaned as he tried to force cooperation from his body.

She helped, and a few moments later he was laying on his stomach while she inspected his back.

"Thank you for shielding me."

"You're welcome. How bad is it?"

"It's…" She brushed her fingertips over his torn back. "I'm not even sure. I need better light."

He cast a mage light and anchored it to her so she could direct it. That was apparently more than he should have done, because he blacked out.

Chapter 24

"Jarl, you dolt!" were the first words he heard when he opened his eyes.

Yes, dolt, Saga echoed.

"Thanks," he muttered, about all he could manage. "Did we get it at least?"

"Yes. Can you wiggle your toes?"

Jarl arched an eyebrow at the unusual request, still not quite feeling up to opening his eyes. "How badly am I hurt," he asked Ima. He was pretty sure it was she who had called him an idiot first.

"Try wiggling your toes, and then we'll tell you."

He sighed and cracked his eyes open, but performed the requested trick.

"Well, not badly then," Ima finally answered. "We weren't sure if we got them all. There were a lot of long shards of dead Crystal in your side. Mostly superficial though you're not going to feel like doing anything too intense for a while."

"Good. Now, why am I a dolt?" His eyes finally focused. Ima and Graesin stared back at him.

"Casting a mage light after all that effort to destroy the Crystal? You're not invincible, you know."

Jarl forced a smile. "I'm getting that impression. Hard to break old habits. I'm still used to having access to large reserves."

Ima's stern expression softened. "I know. Okay, get some more rest."

"Is it gone?" Jarl couldn't hear or feel any trace of the parasite. It was also possible he simply had worn himself out too much to detect the Crystal.

"We did it," Ima said, grinning. "I couldn't have done it without you."

"I don't think I could have done it alone either. Thank you for trusting me, Ima."

She grinned and put her hand on his, squeezing. "Of course, Jarl."

"I'll leave you two alone," Graesin said. "Jarl, rest. As long as you need to. Ima tells me you have quite the battle coming up and you'll need to be at full strength. You may stay as long as you wish."

"Thank you. We'll need to leave as soon as we can." Jarl tried to sit up. Ima pressed down on his chest and he didn't have the energy to argue.

"I'll make sure he stays put at least until I can't overpower him anymore," Ima said to Graesin.

"Good." He stood and left the room.

Jarl's eyelids drooped though he tried to fight it, worried about how much they still had to accomplish.

"Rest, Jarl. I'll keep watch." She leaned over and kissed his forehead.

Shocked, Jarl widened his eyes, but couldn't fight his exhaustion any longer and fell back into a deep sleep.

∞ ∞ ∞

This time when Jarl woke, he was alone. He felt well rested for once. It was difficult to tell how long he had slept as no natural light reached him.

Saga?

174

He almost panicked when she didn't reply. Ima rushed into the room. "She's gone back to the others to check in. Rainer told me you were awake."

He relaxed back onto the cot and took a deep breath. Jerking upright and the deep breath were a mistake. His right side from his hip to his shoulder basically screamed in pain.

"Ow," he groaned as the room swam around him.

"I imagine that hurts quite a bit."

Jarl nodded. "At least my head feels better," he said once the pain quieted.

"The Crystal exploded. You shielded me. Thank you."

"You're welcome." Jarl sighed. Being injured was going to impact his usefulness for a while. At least they knew how to destroy the Crystal now.

Jarl!

The distress in Saga's voice had him jerking upright again. He gasped but managed to get to his feet before Ima could turn and glare at him.

What's wrong? The cool air pricked at his skin, as he let the blanket slide down. Bandages wrapped his torso. He hadn't thought to check, but he was wearing pants, fortunately.

"You don't happen to have one of my spare shirts, do you?" Jarl said, hugging himself against the chill.

Ima crossed her arms. When Jarl didn't lay back down, she went over to a pile of what looked like their tack that lay against one of the rough-cut walls. She dug out a shirt and threw it at him.

He managed to catch it, though moving quickly enough to do so hurt, and he struggled through pulling it on over his head.

"Thanks."

175

"Are you aware of how injured you are yet?" She continued to glare.

"I've got the general idea." He sighed and briefly wished for magical healing. Ima might be able to help him, but she had used as much energy as he had fighting the Crystal and they both needed to conserve their strength.

They poisoned the pie!

"The pie?" he said out loud.

Ima paled. Rainer was probably telling her the same story, or Saga was talking to both of them.

"The world we often use as a waypoint. You've been there once or twice," Ima said.

Jarl did remember Saga bringing him a small hand pie in a basket, and the other time right after he had fought his mother.

His heart sank.

How many more did we lose?

She didn't answer for a minute. He sensed her strengthening her resolve. *Only two. Isolda and Tisk, whom you haven't met. They were with a group and had gone to get the pie. They were sick by the time they returned to the others, so no one else ate it. They couldn't be saved. We need to return. They are convinced we have to strike back now. They need your knowledge.*

Jarl sighed again. "Okay." He glanced at Ima. "We need to see to Una before we leave. If we can reverse what I did to her, we should."

"Are you in any shape to help her?"

Jarl shook his head. "I have to try, though. I don't know that it can be undone."

"Let's go then."

Jarl followed Ima out of the small room and into another of the many hallways. She seemed to know

176

her way around, and Jarl was still somewhat lost so he trailed along behind her, trying to ignore how each step threw jarring pain up his back.

After the short walk, he wondered if he was even going to be able to saddle Saga, let alone get on her back. He knew they would figure something out, but he really wanted to go back to bed. Though he had felt fine, the short walk had sapped his strength. Maybe he would need to hit Ima up for some healing, after they had rested.

Ima knocked on a wooden doorframe someone had fit to the stone.

"Come in," a voice that sounded like Una's called.

They went inside into another small room lined with benches. It looked a lot like the other workshop Jarl and Ima had first met with Graesin in. Bottles cluttered a shelf and some of the workspace.

Una sat on a padded chair and had a book in her lap.

"Jarl, Ima." She smiled more warmly this time. "Excellent job with the Crystal. I hope that knowledge will serve you well in the future."

"It should. If we can destroy it all, many things will change," Jarl said.

Una nodded agreement. "Are you off to return to your war, then?"

"Yes. I wanted to see if I could reverse what I did to you first."

Her eyes widened slightly, and she tilted her chin up. "Please. If you can."

"I don't know that I can, Una, but I need to try."

"Of course. I'm grateful to be alive. I would also be grateful to be whole."

"I understand how you feel," Jarl replied thinking back to his brief captivity on Vanaheim. He dropped into his magesight and studied Una. Right away, he knew he would fail. He had cast the spell blocking her abilities with a great deal of skill, and, with time, he might have been able to unravel it. He didn't have time, or the power he was used to accessing. He wondered if he had unconsciously drawn on the Crystal to cast the spell. The thought made him shudder.

Jarl sank down into another chair and, though he had little confidence, tried to unravel the spell. He worked at it, for what seemed like hours. He would pull at a strand. As soon as he took his attention to another part of the spell, the thread he had worked loose would snap back into place.

Finally, he leaned back in the chair, letting the magesight go and ignoring the headache that followed.

"I can't do it now. I'm not sure if I'll ever be able to, but I promise, when the war with the Vanier is won, or at least at a point where I can step away, I will return and try again." He kept the sorrow out of his voice, barely.

She smiled thinly. "Jarl, it's okay. I really am grateful to be alive and in control of my own mind. There is still much I can do, even without magic. Here." She handed him the book from her lap. "I had thought to decode it, but you will likely have better luck. It's Dvergr in origin."

He studied the book for a moment, opening it and watching the markings swim across the pages as if they were alive. The cover, however, had something on it that looked suspiciously like a Crystal outcropping.

"I think it's Crystal lore. I don't know that for sure. We recovered it from a growth we killed. It had grown all over the cover. Probably attracted to the magic. This part of the cave system wasn't improved by the Dvergr. Other parts you haven't seen were clearly theirs before something, probably the Crystal, happened to them."

"Thank you. Hopefully it has clues to the origin, or at least more useful information. If I can figure out how to read it."

She smiled. "If anyone can, it will be you, Jarl. Now, go to your war and return if you can. And if you are prevented, know that I am grateful to you still."

Jarl stood. "And I to you. What you've taught us is completely invaluable. Please pass on our regards."

Ima said a quick goodbye and then they headed back to the room Jarl had woken in. Ima gathered Jarl's things and handed them to him so he wouldn't have to bend over, then she hefted her own saddle and bags. Jarl used his Farer ability and transported them to Saga and Rainer.

Ima had to saddle his friend too, but he managed to get mounted without help. He patted Saga's shoulder and inhaled her warm, dusty, familiar scent. Despite the pain, he was glad to be in the saddle, and headed back to the Travelers.

Chapter 25

After several stops on different worlds to throw off any trail, Saga and Rainer finally took Jarl and Ima to their destination: a large pasture near a long stone building with a wooden-shingled roof. In the distance Jarl saw more stone buildings, many that looked like houses clustered together. Fields at the end of a harvest season covered the rolling hills, and he saw a tree line in the distance. Livestock grazed in pastures fenced by low stone walls, and smoke rose from a few chimneys. The sun shone high in a deep blue sky with a few puffs of clouds. The scenery was beautiful, but it didn't fill Jarl with any sort of cheer. Mostly he worried for the safety of the people who lived here.

Jarl was feeling pretty beat up by the time they rode up to the long stone building. It was built from rounded stones mortared together and had windows at regular intervals down the side almost like a stable. No horses peeked their heads out to nicker greetings. He did see a flash of movement inside one near the set of double wooden doors that currently stood open to the cool, crisp air.

"Would you like any help?" Ima asked as they dismounted.

"No. Just pretend I'm not injured."

She frowned, but nodded and didn't ask why when Orlinza and William hurried out of the building to meet them.

Jarl was less than pleased to see William. Orlinza's welcoming smile brought an answering one to his own lips.

"So the traitor returns," William said.

Jarl ignored him. Saga whirled and lashed out with a hoof, catching William in the thigh and sending him sprawling to the ground.

Jarl raised his eyebrows, and tried to find something to say, but couldn't think of appropriate words. He certainly wasn't going to reprimand Saga.

Orlinza put her hands on her hips and stared as William picked himself back up. "Are you done?"

William glared at Saga, who stared back, ears pinned.

"You do know she's a trained war horse," Jarl said after a moment. "If she wanted to actually hurt you, she would have."

"And who trained her that way?" William said darkly.

"Well, she chose to take lessons with several arms masters. Fighting is something of a passion for her," Jarl replied.

Saga bobbed her head and continued to glare at William.

He crossed his arms, not saying anything else. That was good enough for Jarl.

"Orlinza, we have news."

"So do we. Come inside. We were in the middle of a planning session for the upcoming assaults. We need information."

"Of course," Jarl said uneasily. Not that he already wasn't a traitor to his people, though he was generally comfortable with the path fate had chosen for him and the choices he had made along that journey. If he helped plan these assaults with all of his knowledge of

182

the areas they would have to hit, he would certainly be the traitor William believed him to be, to the Vanier. If William truly thought he would betray the Travelers, wouldn't he voice some concern?

Tired of the uncertainty, Jarl put it aside and stepped into the stone building. It turned out to be a stable and indoor riding arena. This area must be heavily focused on horses to have such a luxury. Box stalls lined the wall, and a wide walkway ran in front to lead horses, with some tie rails for grooming and tacking. The arena was currently full of a handful of Travelers and some long tables and benches where humans and Alfar mingled. Someone had thrown mats down to make walking on the soft arena floor easier for the two-legged occupants.

Everyone stopped talking and turned to stare as Jarl and the others entered the arena. He tried to walk normally, though his feet dragged with the effort of putting one in front of the other, and his back felt like someone shoved hot brands from a fire into it.

Orlinza strode forward to the head of one of the long tables. "Saga and Jarl say they have news for us. Let's hear theirs and then we can share our plans for the assault and refine them with Jarl's knowledge."

Jarl mentally winced, but he had to help. There was no other option that he could see. Unless they could find the source of the Crystal in the next couple of weeks, which was unlikely, the Vanir had to be hit hard enough that they would leave the Travelers alone for some time while the search continued.

When no one protested, he and Ima walked up to an open spot by the table, Saga and Rainer right behind them.

"We've discovered a way to destroy the Crystal growths with magic. It's not easy but between me and

Ima we managed to destroy the last of a growth on one of the worlds we visited."

"And of course, only you can accomplish this?" William sneered.

"Well, I needed Ima's help to do it. If we had the time, we could probably train others to accomplish the spell, too. Ima knows it as well as I do at this point. I'm just currently better at magic. She'll catch up with some time."

"The point is, we can destroy the Crystal with two methods now, and we should continue to do so," Ima said. "And we will work with any other mages to train them as well.'

"That's excellent news, Jarl and Ima," Orlinza said after a bit more silence from the others. "Now, we've decided that we need to hit Vanaheim and Mageheim to get the Vanier's attention, and then see if we can lure them to a world of our choice, to fight. If we can hit them hard enough, they'll have to spend time regrouping and we can focus on trying to destroy the Crystal. That should always be our main goal, eradicate the parasite."

The others stirred and a few shot uneasy glances at Jarl. He nodded his agreement. He had already come up with similar thoughts; it was simply painful to think about.

"Perhaps we should ask Jarl for the information we need from him, and then plan later," a human woman Jarl thought was named Morgan said.

"Why?" Orlinza asked.

She probably already knew the answer. Why would she bother to ask?

"Because," an Alfar with darker skin and cream-colored hair replied, "wasn't it his fault the Travelers' home world was destroyed? Can we really trust him?"

Saga stamped her foot.

I know his mind. Jarl is not a traitor to us. This discussion ends now! She said it loud enough that everyone at the table winced. A few of the Alfar touched their foreheads as if they had headaches and several of the Travelers shook their heads and flicked their tails in irritation. Not everyone could hear Travelers, but all the beings in the room could.

Jarl leaned his hands on the table and stared at the splintered surface, not sure what to say. Saga was right of course, but no one was going to believe him. Maybe they would believe her.

"How do you plan to assault Mageheim?" he asked. "For that matter, how do you think you will take down the stone walls of Vaneheim? Both are magically protected."

"Jarl, do you remember when you were much younger, and you blew up one of the training labs?" Orlinza smiled

He winced and nodded at the memory. "I'm not the first person to have done that."

"I seem to recall you said it would have been quite a bit worse if you had been in the potions lab. Why is that?"

"Because the other lab had substances that would explode in it, while the lab I was in only had inert substances."

A few of the beings around the table perked up and stared at him. William's eyes widened and he looked excited.

"Are you saying you know how to mix explosives?" William said.

Jarl frowned. "Of course." Then he widened his eyes and nodded. "Yes, of course I do. I just hadn't thought of it in years. No one here knows how?"

"Oh, some of us do, but perhaps not to the same degree that you're familiar," William replied.

"So you want to sneak explosives into Vanaheim and take it down that way?" Jarl thought it might work for the port city. He wasn't so sure about Mageheim.

Jarl, what if we took out the Crystal at Mageheim. Doesn't it power the wards? Saga asked, after sensing his doubts.

"It does," he said aloud, knowing she had spoken to everyone. "And if we take out the wards, the Ovattr will do much of our work for us at Mageheim."

"Ovattr?" Morgan asked.

Orlinza shuddered.

"They are a shadow creature, said to have been created by the Alfar during the war," he said, holding up his hand when a few of the Alfar protested, "that specifically hunt mages. I suspect they were native to our world anyway and it was just another excuse to blame something bad on the Alfar. Regardless, they're difficult to kill, difficult to spot, and seem to exist only to kill people with magical ability. There are a lot of them around Mageheim, and they're hunted regularly. However, I suspect enough will show up that we will have their, uh, aid, in the assault. My suggestion would be, if we can figure out a way to get in and destroy the Crystal growth there, we can then transport explosives to hit the main training building. That will be disruptive enough that we won't have to do much more there. Most of their defenses rely on the wards. The trick will be getting in to destroy the Crystal, and I have no idea how we're going to manage that. Vanaheim, well, if we can sneak in enough wagons of explosives under the guise of caravans and place them around the city, we'll at least be able to hit the city. The palace is really what you need to destroy, but I'm not sure on ideas there either."

"Let's start with explosives," William said. "First, we need materials."

Jarl nodded, feeling grim. "I can certainly help with that." How many people that he cared about were going to be killed in this attack? How many more lives would he be responsible for ending? The trouble was, he couldn't see any other way. The Vanier had to be stopped.

Chapter 26

The next couple of days were chaotic. Saga helped Jarl sneak several people into a couple of different chemical mines his people used. He had never been to them, but it wasn't hard for Saga to use her senses to find the worlds Jarl described. She wondered how the Vanir had first discovered all these other worlds, if their own transportation abilities were so limited. Maybe in time, forgotten Travelers had visited Jarl's people. If there were any keepers of the old stories left, she would have to find them after the war.

Once they had acquired the materials they needed, Jarl instructed the others in their use. They had set up a separate location for mixing the bombs, and all non-essential personnel were kept far away. Saga was only allowed because she wouldn't leave Jarl. She kept close by him in case something happened. Of course, he would probably shield himself, and as many others as he could manage, but she still worried.

Unfortunately, being idle while Jarl worked gave her time to think. What would happen to the people she still cared about on Vanaheim? Weapons Master Beli, and Arms Master Ywain, who had taught her so much about fighting, among others. She couldn't even begin to think about what might happen to Ceridwen and Lady Ailis. Was there something they could do to protect them? Certainly, there was no way to warn Beli and Ywain. Surely, they could protect Ceridwen and Ailis. Couldn't they?

Saga laid her ears back and lashed her tail in frustration.

"What is wrong, my friend?" Jarl said quietly, taking a step back from the table and watching the others work. He folded his arms across his chest and frowned.

When would she see him smile freely again. Ever?

I am worried about Ceridwen and Ailis. Others that we once considered friends may be injured, but those two have done much to help the Alfar and us.

Jarl's shoulders slumped.

Saga was sorry she had brought her worry to Jarl. She could sense his already dark thoughts darken further, and the pain from his injuries pushed back into his awareness as if some mental barrier had dropped.

Sighing, Jarl sank to the trampled grass and leaned against her forelegs with his uninjured side.

I don't know, Saga. I can't think of any way to warn them without alerting the enemy.

Can we steal her away?

Kidnap Ceridwen? No.

Saga got the impression Jarl had already come up with that idea.

There has to be something. Saga huffed in annoyance.

Maybe we can ask Orlinza if she has any ideas, Jarl said.

I will do that as soon as I can.

Jarl leaned his head against her leg and shut his eyes for a moment. She sensed he could have fallen asleep right there. He needed to be alert while the others worked with the chemicals.

Jarl?

Yes, Saga?

Do you regret knowing me?

No! Why would I regret you?

I have led you away from everything you love and dropped you into a war you don't really want.

I love you, Saga. And I still have you. That's what is most important.

She nuzzled his hair and noted it was getting rather shaggy. *When this is all over, maybe you can find Ceridwen again.*

Jarl shook his head. *I doubt it will be over in time for anything between us to work out, Saga. Maybe there will be someone else, someday, but probably not.*

She couldn't seem to say the right thing to Jarl, so she fell silent and they watched the others work.

Finally, it was time for a break, and she insisted Jarl come away. He needed rest.

He threw his arm over her withers and leaned against her as she led him to the small home they shared with Orlinza and Ima. If she could convince him to let the others work without him, he might actually be able to get some real rest, as tired as he was.

He stumbled into the house, aided by Saga only for both of them to be stopped short by Orlinza.

"Jarl, what is wrong?"

"I haven't recovered from all the magic use yet."

That wasn't really a lie, Saga knew. Of course, it wasn't the full story either.

"You are walking around like you're an old man instead of a young and highly trained fighter. What is wrong?"

Jarl shrugged. "I took a little damage when we destroyed the Crystal. It's not bad."

Orlinza's eyebrows rose. "Show me."

191

"Linny..."

"Now." She pointed toward Jarl's room.

Saga nickered in sympathy and nudged Jarl's shoulder. He sighed and headed for his room, tugging at the laces at his throat so he could pull his shirt off.

He managed to get half out of his shirt, but his injured side didn't cooperate. Saga grabbed his shirt with her teeth and pulled, helping him slide out of it. The bandages he had wrapped around his torso earlier in the day were stained with sweat and some blood.

Saga snorted and shook her head. *That doesn't look good.*

It does not feel good either.

Orlinza practically growled at Jarl as she unwrapped the bandages. "We have medicine, Jarl. Has Ima tried to heal you?"

"Ima has needed rest as much as I have."

"Jarl, we need you in one piece." She pointed at his bed and he sighed and laid down on his chest.

"Saga, please get Ima."

Saga tossed her head and left the small cottage, heading for the barn where Ima was with the others.

She picked up an easy canter, not wanting to alarm anyone. Jarl wasn't in immediate danger, but he really did need to do something about his wounds. They weren't healing quickly.

Ima and the others sat around a diagram of Mageheim that Orlinza had provided, probably trying to figure out how to attack the Crystal.

Ima, would you please come with me. Orlinza wants you.

"Of course, Saga. Please excuse me."

The others were engrossed in their discussion and barely noticed when she left.

"What's wrong?"

Jarl's wounds are worse. She wants you to try to heal them.

Ima sighed. "I'm not sure I know how, but I'll certainly try."

I believe she will use some medicine, too.

"That would be wise."

Before long they were back in the small house and Ima sat down next to Jarl. "I'll do what I can," she said.

"Don't wear yourself out," Jarl said quietly. "We need to be rested if we're going to take out the Crystal at Mageheim."

"Jarl, if you're not recovered, I'm going to have to find someone else to help me, so shut up and let me work." Ima put her hand on his shoulder and shut her eyes, muttering something about stubborn humans.

Saga wanted to nicker laughter, but she was worried about Jarl and refrained. It wasn't like him to simply ignore something that was bothering him. He should have tried to get some sort of medication earlier instead of letting it go like he had. Saga should have paid more attention to her friend too, but Orlinza was helping him now.

Ima concentrated on Jarl for a few minutes and Orlinza rubbed some salve on his back.

"Okay, Jarl, get some sleep. We'll check on you again in a few hours."

He mumbled agreement, already falling asleep.

I will watch him, Saga said.

Orlinza patted her shoulder as she squeezed past the Traveler. Ima stayed for a few minutes longer watching Jarl before she too left.

Saga, alone with her worry, sighed and settled in to wait and guard her friend. What else could she do?

Chapter 27

It took a couple of days, but Jarl finally felt nearly human again. By the time he managed to get out of bed, Saga had squeezed her way into the small house.

Are you feeling better?

"Yes, my friend. Thank you."

We have a plan for Ceridwen and Lady Ailis.

"I'm not going to like it, am I?" He could tell by the tone of her voice.

No. We need to kidnap them.

Jarl sighed. "Great."

It's the only way to warn them, keep them safe, and prevent any chance of them warning others. For something this major, Ceridwen might not cooperate.

"I know. She cares about her people."

You and I will go get her. Ima wanted to come as well, but we can't risk all of our mages.

"Do you know where she's at?"

No. We will start at Skeradder. We will have to hope she is there, because we won't have much time. Getting her out of Vanaheim could be impossible.

Jarl ground his teeth, though he agreed. "Have you figured out a plan to deal with the Crystal at Mageheim too?"

Yes. It is also very dangerous. We are gathering all the powder we have. It isn't much, and it probably won't be enough to completely destroy the Crystal. William will sneak in and hit Crystal. Once it is weakened, we believe it will take down the wards, or at least make them breachable. Then you and Ima will tie yourselves to your saddles and attack the Crystal with magic. You will not fall off because we cannot lose either of you and we know the Crystal will fight back.

The two attacks will happen at the same time. Orlinza is helping to coordinate both as she knows both cities. We do not need to worry about the attack on Vanaheim.

"Please tell me the main targets are the walls and the rulers. The civilians..." He groaned.

Yes, the attack is focusing on taking out military targets. Unfortunately, it will go badly for anyone there. I don't see how we can avoid it.

Jarl leaned his forehead against his friend's shoulder. "We really did bring this upon ourselves, didn't we?"

Yes.

"Okay. Let's find William."

Perhaps first you should shower.

Jarl frowned.

I also would like to be clean.

"Of course."

And we need to plan Ceridwen's... Saga shifted. *Rescue.*

Jarl knuckled his eyes. How had his life had come to this? Then he squared his shoulders. It was decided, and there was nothing left to do but carry out his tasks. His mother had destroyed far more than he and the Travelers were about to, and while it wasn't exactly comforting, it made the situation hurt less.

At least he felt better. Ima's healing and a few days of rest had done wonders.

A Traveler named Aoife joined Jarl and Saga. She was tall and black with a white blaze down her face and three white slashes across her hindquarters. She wore a saddle, but she kept looking at it like she had never worn one before.

Have you carried a rider before? Saga asked.

Aoife laid her ears flat and shook her head. *No, but it will be okay.*

"You've never had anyone on your back?"

Aoife lowered her head and shook it.

"It's okay, Aoife, maybe you should let me get on for a minute just so you have experienced it once before we're in a potentially dangerous situation," Jarl said.

The mare studied Jarl out of one eye before flicking both ears toward him. *This is wise.*

Jarl thought back to the first time he got on Saga's back and smiled at the memory. He came over to her side. "The first thing to remember is that while both Ceridwen and Ailis are accomplished riders, they're used to horses. They may try to direct you. Also, they're not going to think twice about touching you without first making sure it's okay. May I?" He held his hand over her shoulder.

Yes.

He patted her, then rubbed his hand up her neck. She shivered under his touch, but stood still, neck turned slightly toward him watching, her eye and ear both focused on what he did.

"Okay, I'm going to tug on your mane. You'll have to get used to that quickly." He gave a quick, but reasonably gentle jerk.

Aoife snorted. *It is not as if it hurts. It just feels strange.*

"Yes." Jarl spent a minute just walking around Aoife and patting her in all the normal places humans touched horses on a regular basis. He even tugged on her tail.

Aoife laid her ears back for a minute. She flicked them up again when Saga snorted laughter.

Jarl checked the girth on the saddle, found it tight, and tugged on one of the stirrups. "Okay, try to stand still please, while I get on."

Okay.

Jarl put his foot in the stirrup, grabbed Aoife's mane and smoothly mounted. The Traveler snorted, ears flicking out to the side, eyes going wide.

"Easy there."

She took a deep breath and Saga nickered in sympathy. *Even though Jarl and I had planned our first ride together for years, I still shied the first time he got on me. It was silly, but it is a different feeling.*

Aoife took another deep breath. *It is. I'm going to walk.*

"Okay."

The Traveler took a few tentative steps and after a moment she walked confidently while Jarl balanced on her back, lightly holding her mane.

May I try to canter?

"Sure."

If you hurt my human, I will be upset, Saga said, tail lashing.

"Easy, Saga. She's not going to do anything to hurt me." Jarl patted Aoife's neck before squeezing his legs.

What!

"I told you, they'll try to direct you. Even between experienced Travelers and riders, we use the same signals to communicate. It is often faster than thought."

She took another deep breath, shook her head, and seemed to laugh at herself. *Do it again.*

Jarl signaled for a canter and the Traveler moved out. For a moment, her gait was choppy, then she settled and came smoothly to a halt next to Saga.

I am ready. Thank you, Jarl.

"You're welcome." Jarl dismounted Aoife and got on Saga.

As the two Travelers turned to leave, William and Orlinza approached.

"Can you do this?" William said when they got closer.

"Yes," Jarl replied.

"Then get out of here so we can all rest easier." William glared.

Jarl tilted his head. "What do you mean?" He ignored the glare, that's the only way William ever looked at him.

"There's a bit of worry you'll change your mind with your Lady in danger," he said bluntly.

Orlinza frowned. However, she didn't contradict William.

"Ah." The thought hadn't actually crossed his mind, but now that it was pointed out to him, the worry seemed reasonable. "I see."

"Jarl, we're moving our base. William, Brigid, and Dance will remain to guide you to the world we have chosen for Ceridwen to hide on. Once she is settled, William will fill you in on the rest of the plan," Orlinza held out her hand and Jarl took it. "Be careful. She may be guarded."

"I will. You as well. Hopefully we will see each other again soon."

Orlinza nodded. Jarl caught a hint of uncertainty in her expression and it worried him.

Saga stepped forward and folded Orlinza into the Traveler's equivalent of a hug.

They turned away from each other and Saga and Aoife trotted away from Orlinza and William.

Jarl looked over his shoulder and waved. Orlinza waved back. William continued to glare.

Take us home, Jarl said to Saga. For Vanaheim would always be home to at least some part of him.

Chapter 28

Somehow the Travelers timed their arrival so that they stepped out of the *Through* into darkness. Saga and Aoife stood still, and everyone listened.

Everyone tensed, ready to flee, when a branch snapped nearby.

Jarl, barely daring to breath, listened.

It is a deer. I can smell it, Saga said.

Slowly, Jarl let out his breath. Not quite ready to make any noise he didn't have to. *Okay, contact Ceridwen if you can, please.*

I will try.

Saga was quiet for a while, and Jarl stayed tense, ready to cast a defensive spell, or for Saga to turn and bolt at any moment.

Finally, Saga sighed out a breath, an equine sign of relaxation. *She and Lady Ailis are coming, but she cautions that she will likely never be able to sneak out again as it is likely she will get caught when she returns.*

Do you think they are truly alone? Jarl asked.

She believes they are, but I would be extremely careful.

Aoife, could you move off in the distance a short way, just in case?

Yes, Jarl.

The black Traveler made little sound as she moved away from them, and Jarl soon lost track of her in the darkness.

They waited for a tense twenty minutes or so, before he heard the quiet sounds of someone moving through the woods. She wasn't loud, but she wasn't as quiet as someone well practiced at stalking through the forest would have been.

Aoife, do you hear anyone else? Jarl directed that thought at both Travelers.

No.

"Jarl, what are you doing here?" Ceridwen asked when she was standing next to Saga's shoulder.

Saga, do they smell right? When Conor snuck me out of the castle, he disguised me as Ceridwen.

It's them, unless they managed to disguise their smell, too. I don't think Conor would have thought of that, however, or easily been able to duplicate them to the level I can smell.

It's not something we learn.

"I'm, um…" What should he say? He really didn't want to outright admit he was kidnapping them unless it came down to it. He sighed. "You two have to come with us. It's not safe here and we want to get you somewhere protected."

"Jarl, I'm not leaving Vanaheim."

"I am prepared to force you to leave, Ceridwen. It's temporary. You'll be returned after a while. We just want you safe. Many of us want you safe. The Alfar especially know what you've done for them."

Ceridwen was silent for a moment. "Jarl, we can't leave. There is still so much to be done here."

"Ceridwen. You have to, and we need to go now in case you were followed."

Jarl!

Aoife, do you hear anything?

I thought I heard something. I'm not sure now.
The black Traveler's voice wavered uncertainly.

Safer to assume you did, Saga said.

Saga nudged Ceridwen. *Come with us so we don't have to fight you.*

"Do you mean fight me now, or fight me later?"

"Both," Jarl muttered. He held out his hand.

"You would force us to go with you?" Lady Ailis finally spoke.

"Yes."

"Lady Ceridwen, we should go with them. We can't win a fight with Jarl, and if we were followed it will go badly for everyone. Saga will make sure we get home when it is safe."

If not me, then one of the others.

"You will ride Aoife."

The black Traveler came to stand beside Lady Ailis. Lady Ailis didn't wait for Ceridwen to decide, she mounted quickly.

Go.

Aoife, already nervous, didn't need any encouragement. She turned and trotted into the *Through.*

"I'm not sure I'll ever get used to that," Ceridwen said and held out her hand.

Her hand trembled in Jarl's. She put her foot in the stirrup and he pulled her up behind him.

This time even he heard the branch snap.

Saga didn't even wait for a suggestion. She bolted into the *Through* and Jarl thought he heard swearing behind them as they landed on a day-lit world.

Ceridwen gasped, and once Jarl's eyes adjusted, he saw Saga had brought them to a tropical beach. Water

203

hissed along the sand, lapping at her hooves. Aoife and Lady Ailis waited in the distance.

Cerdiwen tightened her grip around Jarl's waist as Saga cantered toward the other Traveler. He tried not to think about how amazing it was to have Ceridwen's arms wrapped around him.

"Lady Ceridwen, this is so amazing," Ailis said, laughing. "Is this your base?"

"Yes," Jarl lied, hoping nothing bad would happen. "It's not far from here."

Saga's ears flicked at the lie, but she understood.

Jarl opened himself to his magesight and looked at Ailis. She had several different tracking spells on her, and he was sure Ceridwen had the same.

"Okay, both of you dismount for a moment."

The two Travelers moved out of the surf but stayed on the packed sand as the women dismounted.

"What's wrong, Jarl?" Ceridwen asked.

"Both of you have tracking spells on you. I need to remove them. Quickly because I'm sure the others won't be far behind."

You will not enjoy the experience if we are chased, Saga said. *It is not a comfortable way to travel the* Through.

Jarl quickly unraveled the spells on the two women, though he was relieved to see that they both were who they appeared to be. Then he turned his magesight on himself and the Travelers. None of the spells had attached to anyone else. That was an oversight the Vanier would regret. Some spells could be made to be sticky. Or perhaps they simply hadn't been touched.

Once he was convinced they were clear of spells, he held his hand out for Ceridwen again.

"I thought you said this was your base?" Ailis frowned at Jarl.

"I lied. It's not safe to come directly to any world when you might be followed."

"I see. Probably wise." Her expression soured.

"Why not simply tell us that?" Ceridwen said sharply.

"Because, magic is powerful, and I had to make sure nothing would happen if I said we were at our final destination." Jarl sighed.

Both women shared a look before they turned toward the Travelers.

Ceridwen accepted Jarl's hand and mounted as did Lady Ailis.

The back of Jarl's neck tingled. "Go!"

The Travelers both leapt into the *Through*.

Ceridwen clung to him, and he could only imagine how Lady Ailis felt, though she had the benefit of being the only one on her Traveler.

Saga and Aoife bounced off several worlds, It wasn't as bad as when they were being actively chased. He hoped they had exercised enough caution in their escape.

When they came out in the pasture it was late afternoon. A quiet breeze ruffled the grasses. Brigid, Dance, William, and a Traveler Jarl didn't know waited.

"Lady Ceridwen, Lady Ailis, please, we need you to change your clothing and leave anything you carry behind."

Jarl helped Ceridwen off Saga. She glanced up at him, and though he hadn't been aware of that part of the plan, he nodded his agreement.

Ceridwen and Lady Ailis went with Brigid and returned after a few minutes wearing clothing more typical of the humans and Alfar who partnered with the Travelers instead of their more refined dresses.

"Trousers will be easier to ride in," Ceridwen said a little tightly. She was clearly unhappy with the situation.

"I imagine so," Jarl said. He held out his hand, and though she took it, the hesitation before she did so tugged at his heart.

"Jarl, I can't believe you're going to attack Vanaheim," Ceridwen said.

William shot Jarl a dark look and Ceridwen glared back at him.

"He didn't say that you were going to. It's the only reason I can think of that he would tell me Vanaheim was no longer safe for us." The anger in her voice cut Jarl to his core.

"Did anyone tell you what my mother did to the Travelers' home world?"

"No."

"If you knew, you might understand."

"Then tell me."

"We have to go," William snapped. "You can continue this reunion when we're safe."

"Where are we going?" Ceridwen asked.

"I don't know," Jarl answered. "We'll find out when we get there."

Before she could ask another question, the Travelers trotted into the *Through* and the vibrant colors of yet another world Jarl would likely never see again ran like wet ink around them.

Chapter 29

They finally stopped Traveling on a world with silver-barked trees whose red leaves tinkled metallically in the wind. The sunlight filtered through the canopy and Saga thought it was near noon by the position of the sun in the sky. She was exhausted but on edge. She could feel Ceridwen's anger, and by the tense way Jarl sat he could, too. There wasn't much to be done about it, however.

This world does not have Crystal, and they shouldn't be able to follow us here. We don't think the Vanier have ever been here. It's quite distant from Vanaheim.

"So you're abandoning us on a distant world alone?" Fear tinged Ceridwen's voice.

No. Many of the Alfar are here, and they will see to your care.

"It really is for the best," Lady Ailis said. "We can't do anything while they're at war anyway, and they will return us when it is safe."

"You seem rather cheerful about all of this," Ceridwen said.

"I'm not complaining about not being in the middle of a war. Vanaheim can take care of itself for a while. After what they did to the Alfar, well, I'm not so sure I want to be there anyway."

Ceridwen sighed. "Very well. Take us to our prison."

Lady Ailis gave Ceridwen a sharp look, and Brigid traded a concerned glance with William.

William and the Traveler he rode, a dapple gray named Ronny, led the way.

They wound down a small cart trail, rutted from years of use. The air was warm and a touch humid, but not uncomfortable, though Saga sweated a little.

It didn't take long before they came to a small cluster of wooden cabins. The wood all shone silver like the trees that surrounded them. The red roofs looked like someone had woven together the broad metal leaves from the trees into some sort of large dragon-scale covering, and the scent of wood smoke and cooking food filled the air.

A few Travelers with their young grazed in a clearing nearby and several Alfar worked in a garden near the center of the clearing the cabins circled.

Saga nickered a greeting when Niamh and Faiz came out to welcome them.

"Hello, Lady Ceridwen, Lady Ailis. Would you please come with us?" Faiz bowed slightly.

Jarl helped Ceridwen down and Lady Ailis dismounted as well. Both followed the Alfar. Only Lady Ailis spared a backward glance for the group.

"I hear something happened to the Travelers' home world," Ceridwen said to Faiz as they walked away.

"A terrible tragedy."

Saga knew that the Alfar would tell Ceridwen what had happened, and then maybe she would understand. Saga could only hope.

"Well, that went well," Brigid said once Ceridwen was out of hearing range.

Dance snorted laughter.

"Yes, well, I'm not sure we could expect more. No one likes being kidnapped," Jarl said curtly. "Are we staying here, or are we continuing on?"

"We're leaving," William said.

Jarl relaxed his tense shoulders and Saga sighed in relief. Carrying two tense riders was hard on her back. He patted her shoulder.

Are you okay, my friend?

Yes, you? she replied.

No, but there's no help for it.

Saga followed when Ronny led the way back down the cart path. Brigid and Dance rode up beside them, saying nothing, and Jarl ignored them.

I hope that's not the last time I see her.

Saga wasn't sure she was meant to hear Jarl's anguished thought, so she didn't reply, but his pain tore at her. She would make it better. Somehow.

After a short time trotting down the cart path, they entered the *Through*. The possible destinations filled Saga with longing to visit each and every one. She could shift her focus slightly to one or the other and understand enough about the world to know the type of environments it contained, and if she concentrated more closely, she could tell much about where she would exit the *Through*.

Finally, they came out on a world Saga knew was near Vanaheim. She could sense from Jarl's surface thoughts that he had been here a time or two himself. The ground crunched under her feet and blue Crystal outcroppings glittered in the harsh sunlight, covering crumbling rock and dominating the landscape.

Saga shook, trying to get the prickly feeling of being around that much Crystal off her skin. Jarl put a hand on her shoulder.

"The others will meet us here shortly," William said. "Dance assures me that you can get to Vanaheim very quickly from this world. The plan is for me to go alone and sneak in to Mageheim with a caravan. We've been watching, and there is one approaching so it shouldn't take long. You and the others will wait here until Ronny tells you that I'm in. That will be the signal to begin both attacks. Once I weaken the Crystal, Jarl you and Ima will destroy it. We've got a few other plans for attacking the structure. Your only job is to destroy the Crystal at Mageheim and get out. As much as I'd just as soon be rid of you, I know we need you and there is too much risk with you staying on Vanaheim for long. Ima will be here shortly. Do you understand?" William said curtly.

"Yes. We will destroy the Crystal and get off Vanaheim." Jarl's voice sounded even more wooden than what was becoming normal.

"Can you do it?"

"Yes, William, I can destroy the Crystal at Mageheim. With Ima's help. We'll get in and get out. You just make sure you can do your part and get the wards down enough for us to get in," Jarl snapped.

"Will you do it?" He crossed his arms and glared at Jarl.

"Yes, William. I will. The Crystal is a terrible parasite." Jarl curled his hands into fists in her mane and all the tension he had shed was back.

"After the attack, return to this world. Dance and Brigid will take you to the world we're preparing for our final battle. We're going to need your help to lure your people to us. We can do it without. It'll be easier if we can dangle you as bait. They've also got armor and weapons."

I would very much like armor for the fight.

210

"Me too," Jarl said.

"We won't have much time to rest from the attack. We want them mad and we don't want them to think much about what they're doing when they chase you," William said.

"That's fine," Jarl replied.

"I'm heading out. Be ready to move. It'll be a couple of hours." Ronny turned and cantered into the *Through* with William.

Saga sighed.

"Brigid, where should we wait?" Jarl looked at the other Vanier.

"Over there. We dropped a small cache of food for everyone."

Oat cakes?

Brigid laughed. "Yes. We have some of those, too."

Good.

They followed Brigid and Ima, and Rainer joined them shortly.

"Saga, I thought you might want this," Ima said holding out Saga's short sword with its leather wrapped handle.

Yes, thank you Ima.

"Thank you," Jarl echoed. He took it from Ima and fastened it to Saga's saddle.

"And I have some straps for the saddles so we can tie ourselves on. We do not want to be left behind and we don't want to cause our Travelers to get caught."

"You don't have to convince me," Jarl said. "This won't be easy, even if William manages to weaken it ahead of time. It's going to take a lot out of us. Maybe they will let us rest for a day at least, before the final battle."

"I believe that is part of the plan," Brigid added.

"Well, let's figure out how these straps work. Saga, eat up."

You don't have to tell me again, she dug into the forage and oat cakes that had been brought for the Travelers while Jarl and Ima experimented with the straps.

All too soon, Saga felt the touch of Ronny's mind as he Traveled back to the world they were on.

It's time to go.

Jarl and Ima mounted and secured the straps from their belts to the saddles.

Saga didn't let herself have time to feel nervous, she just headed into the *Through* as soon as Jarl, Rainer, and Ima were ready. It was time to really fight back.

Chapter 30

Jarl didn't let himself have time to think past the mild surprise that Saga and Rainer brought them out into the courtyard at Mageheim and not outside the walls. William must have damaged the wards more completely that Jarl had expected. Or it was another trap.

The last thought faded away as Jarl heard shouting, the clash of steel on steel, and other sounds of people trying to kill each other. Jarl didn't really want to know the details of how William and the others had gotten so many people onto Vanaheim to fight

Gritting his teeth and wishing he could help, he instead turned his focus onto his mission. Saga and Rainer raced toward the main building where the Crystal was housed. Armored humans wearing the Crystal insignia on their breastplates fought with a couple of men wearing boiled leather armor on the main steps, blocking their entrance.

Saga. See if you can reach those men and get them to disengage so we can get through.

I will do my best. Rainer, once we get inside, keep in mind the footing is slick. It's all stone.

Jarl didn't hear the other Traveler reply, or what Saga said to the combatants ahead. After a moment one of the men shoved his opponent back and grabbed his companion. They moved out of the way just as

Saga and Rainer charged forward, surprising the guards. They fell under Saga's and Rainer's hooves as the Travelers charged into them, and Jarl really hoped that he didn't know either of the guards, though he probably did. He shoved open the main doors with a burst of magic and they entered the main hall.

Saga didn't comment, but he could feel her tension through their bond.

The Travelers' hooves clattered across the smooth stone floors, and Jarl could feel Saga's muscles tense to keep herself from slipping as they ran.

The stained glass threw colorful beams of light and illuminated the halls he had spent so much time in not all that long ago. The Crystal insignia dominated the artwork. Other tapestries flashed by as well. Jarl knew most of them well and didn't waste much time thinking about them as they galloped toward the outcropping of Crystal.

The small group didn't meet any resistance until they arrived at the Crystal. Two mages, one Jarl recognized as Master Fridge the Head Master's second in command, the other mage was Master Iverson from Vanaheim.

The Crystal itself was cracked and oozing blue liquid. Unfortunately, it still pulsed with life and Jarl could feel its distress even though he no longer possessed rings made of the same material.

Master Frige and Master Iverson turned at the sound of hooves thudding down the hallway and glared. Both raised their hands. Jarl sat up in the saddle and cast as strong a shield spell as he could manage.

The spells the other mages threw at them splattered in a spray of color across the invisible shield, momentarily blocking their view.

Ima wants you to drop the shield.

Jarl didn't take the time to question his student; he did as asked.

Before the sparkles could clear from his vision, Ima shouted and threw a spell back at the other mages.

Jarl raised his shield as his vision cleared. Both Master Frige and Master Iverson were sprawled out in front of the Crystal. Jarl turned and glanced at Ima. She smiled and shrugged as they skidded to a halt, both Traveler's haunches sinking almost to the ground as they tried to stop their headlong charge before they crashed into the bleeding parasite.

Jarl glanced at the masters. They both looked knocked out for the moment. Then he saw William, also sprawled nearby. Dead or unconscious.

First, they had to finish the Crystal.

The ground trembled and dust sprinkled down from the ceiling. Dust motes sparkled in the light of the stained glass and cracks split the plaster walls.

"What was that?" Ima asked.

"Best guess? The labs just blew up. Come on, let's finish this. If we can, we need to get William when we're done." Jarl pointed at Ima's confused look.

"Shards," she whispered. "We're under very strict orders not to dismount."

"Let's get the Crystal first. He may not even be alive. Do you want to lead?"

"No, Jarl, you do it."

He nodded and dropped fully into his magesight while Saga and Rainer kept watch. He felt Ima lend her strength to him, and he began to shape the spell.

The Crystal must have had some idea what he was up to, because it pulsed, and Jarl thought he sensed alarm.

It sent bursts of energy to the fallen mages.

Jarl, they're waking up!

The only thing he could do was shape the spell more quickly. He wove his hands in the needed patterns. Through the magical energies that connected him to Ima, he could feel her growing fear. They were both effectively helpless against the other mages while Jarl worked unless he dropped the spell.

William, wake up! Jarl heard Saga shout.

He twisted the threads of the spell energy into the final shape just as the other two mages scrambled to their feet.

He released the spell right as Saga reared.

Jarl's spell struck true, and the Crystal screamed in agony.

Jarl clutched his head and thanked whoever had the foresight to convince the mages to tie themselves to their saddles as he would have been on the ground without them. As it was, he had to scramble to regain his balance.

The two Vanier mages clutched their heads, and Ima sat slumped in her saddle, though she perked up quickly.

Shaking his head to help clear his vision, Jarl saw that the mages' rings had shattered, too. He also saw William was up, but staggering.

"Come on!" He pointed at William, and Saga sensed his intention.

She raced over to William, and Jarl, though the effort cost him after destroying the Crystal, used magic to help heave William across Saga's rump. She snorted but didn't object as they turned and ran for the exit.

The Crystal is gone. We can leave from here, Saga said in warning before she and Rainer raced into the *Through.*

Chapter 31

They bounced back to the dry, dusty world, puffs of dust marking their passage as they raced toward the small camp where Brigid waited on Dance.

William grunted with each stride, but he didn't complain, and Jarl managed to maintain the magic that held William to Saga's back.

"Where is Ronny?" Brigid shouted when they came into view.

William groaned and Jarl released the magic.

The man slid bonelessly off Saga's back and crumpled to the ground. Before anyone could get too worried about the other Traveler, Ronny burst out of the *Through* and went over to William, nuzzling him.

Jarl wondered if Ronny had chosen William as a partner—or just concerned because he felt responsible. It wasn't truly Jarl's business though, so he didn't ask.

William groaned before hooking his hand on Ronny's stirrup and pulling himself to his feet.

"That is the most uncomfortable way to ride," he muttered as he leaned against the dapple-gray Traveler.

"Sorry," Jarl said.

"I think I can manage to forgive you," William said sounding a little better. "Especially if we get out of here."

"We should go," Brigid said.

Jarl sagged in the saddle; the rush of energy and excitement that had sustained him leaving abruptly. He thought he felt Saga tremble. She shook her head and felt steady again.

Brigid dismounted and helped William climb into the saddle, then she jumped back onto Dance before entering the *Through.* This time Jarl didn't think anyone followed. They must have been busy dealing with the chaos at Vanaheim and Mageheim. He tried to feel bad, and just couldn't manage the energy to do so.

After a relatively short hop, considering most of the running away they had been doing recently, they came out of the *Through* in a lush green field.

The Travelers all nickered in appreciation of the grasses that brushed against their legs, anticipating a snack relatively soon.

Jarl looked around. The green field was bordered on one side by rocky cliffs and pine trees dotted the landscape. They air was cool and crisp, and they were at a relatively high elevation in a mountainous valley. The terrain dropped away, dotted with boulders and other rocky outcroppings behind them, even as it rose before them. There was plenty of room for a battle of the sort that would soon occur, and Jarl winced at the anticipated damage to the beautiful scenery. Though the sun shone high in the vibrant blue sky, Jarl's shoulders sagged with exhaustion and he wished for sleep soon. He needed to know the coming plan, but he suspected the elements were already in place.

"Where are we?" Jarl asked Brigid.

"Glynneath," she replied.

"Ah." The choice of location made a lot of sense, and they must have talked with Brigid to choose it, though how she had known about it, Jarl wasn't sure.

There wasn't much on this planet, but he knew there was a strong Crystal presence in the lower elevations. That would give the Vanier mages an advantage, but they had the advantage anyway. It wasn't far from Vanaheim as the Travelers saw things, and it wouldn't be hard for him to use his own ability to get back and forth as well. It was a reasonably ideal location, especially since the Travelers had been here long enough to set up their fortifications. He anticipated they had anyway.

"Jarl, we've set this up to look like a temporary encampment," Brigid said while they rode to a series of tents. "We only told a few people, other than those here, where the battle would be for security measures. Even Orlinza doesn't know. We believe that between hitting Mageheim and Vanaheim they will be too damaged to hurt us for a long time. Our main goal here is to take out as many mages as we can. That's really the key to keeping ourselves safe."

He had already come to the same conclusion. "It won't be easy, as you know."

"We're hoping you and Ima can cast the Crystal destroying spell one more time and take out their rings. That will even things up quite a bit." Brigid studied Jarl while she said this.

Jarl raised his eyebrows. That was a brilliant idea.

Ima gasped. "We should have thought of that sooner."

"To be fair, we did just discover the spell," Jarl said.

"True."

"When you two do the spell, we will use the distraction to kill as many mages as we can target. We have archers with plenty of arrows. Then it'll be up to you and Ima and a few of the others to battle the mages while we handle the rest of the troops."

"That is a solid plan," Jarl said. He couldn't think of anything better.

"Good. Now you four get some rest. Sleep as long as you need to. We have a little time before we'll be ready." Brigid gestured toward a tent with no gear outside.

Ima and Jarl glanced at each other before they climbed wearily off their Travelers.

"William, go get some rest as well. And medical attention," Brigid ordered.

William gave Jarl one last considering look before he nodded at the mage and left with Ronny.

Jarl suspected that was as close as he would ever get to a friendly acknowledgement from that man, but that was okay. It was an improvement.

"We will have armor and food brought for the Travelers. Go sleep."

"Thanks," Jarl said, feeling all the aches and pains from the last few weeks catching up to him as he pulled at the buckles on Saga's tack.

She nickered and nudged his shoulder, saying nothing.

"Hey, you're injured. Are you okay?" He rubbed a burned patch on Saga's chest.

I am fine, Jarl. It is minor.

"Brigid, could you bring some ointment?"

"Yes." She rode away on Dance, and by the time Jarl had Saga's tack off, an unfamiliar Alfar returned. The Alfar had pale skin and short white hair, with glassy blue eyes. He carried a sword at his hip and a bow and quiver slung across his back. More importantly, he had some salve.

"I'm Finn," he said. "Saga, may I take care of your wound?"

She bobbed her head. *Jarl, they will take care of me. Go sleep.*

Though reluctant to leave his partner, he could barely keep his eyes open. He staggered into the tent. Someone had laid out blankets in the narrow space and Ima was already passed out on one side. Jarl managed to kick off his boots before he collapsed next to her, too tired to even worry about the tight sleeping arrangements.

Chapter 32

Jarl woke later to darkness. Sometime while they both slept, Ima must have curled up against him, possibly for warmth as it was a bit chilly except where he could feel her pressed up against his back. Her arm was over his waist and her breath tickled his neck.

He didn't move, not wanting to disturb her and strangely comforted by her presence. It was the first time he had woken cuddled up with anyone but Saga.

Saga pushed her head through the tent flaps, briefly showing a moonlit landscape behind her. *She likes you.*

I'm sure she was just cold, Jarl replied.

Saga nickered softly and left the tent. *Perhaps. Go back to sleep.*

Jarl wanted to protest that he was fine, but it was the middle of the local night and his eyelids drooped before he could finish the thought.

The next time he woke, sunlight filtered through the gap in the tent flap. Ima still lay curled up around him. He could tell she was awake by her breathing.

"I'm sorry, Jarl," she said quietly. "I didn't want to wake you by moving."

Ima moved her arm and leaned away from him, leaving Jarl feeling alone. He rolled over, propping himself up on his elbow and looking at his friend. He smiled. "It's okay. It gets chilly in the mountains at night."

Jarl almost thought Ima blushed.

"I, uh…" She brushed some of her hair out of her face. "Well, I just wanted to say it's been an honor to know you and study magic with you." She looked down. "You know, just in case we don't make it."

Jarl put his hand on Ima's forearm and squeezed. "Yes, it has been wonderful to get to know you. Hopefully we both survive then we'll get to learn even more from each other."

She smiled and studied him for a moment before leaning forward.

Jarl's breath caught as she pressed her lips to his. For a moment, he froze, not quite sure what to do.

Kiss her back, silly, Saga interrupted his confusion.

It seemed like good advice, so he responded.

Ima pulled him close, pressed against his chest, lips warm against his. Kissing Ima was different than kissing Ceridwen the few times he had. Ima was assertive as she wrapped herself around Jarl.

He trailed his hands over her shoulders, down her muscular back, holding her tightly.

After a few minutes she broke away, smiling. "We can continue this discussion later."

Jarl, still shocked, nodded and watched as she scooted to the edge of the pile of blankets they had slept on and pulled on her boots. She left the tent and he continued to stare at the gap between the two flaps.

Saga finally stuck her head in and nickered laughter. *I told you she liked you.*

"I…" He didn't even know what to say, so he shut his mouth and put his boots on. *What do I do?* Jarl asked finally.

Right now, you survive the coming battle. After, well, you will just have to see what happens. There is no point in thinking about either Ima or Ceridwen right now. She had clearly sensed his thoughts stray toward his former betrothed. She was right though. He could deal with all of that if they survived.

Jarl groaned and climbed out of the tent. Saga moved out of his way so he could stand and stretch stiff muscles.

"How are you feeling?"

I feel good. Rested. Ready for the fight. Saga nickered and reared a little as if to demonstrate her fitness. *Tack me, please. I want to make sure everything fits before we go fetch the Vanier to this fight.*

Jarl obliged his friend, fitting on the padded chest plate someone had left for Saga, along with her normal gear. He left off the saddlebags. They wouldn't need any of that in the coming struggle. He had a minute to wish he could go check in and see if their custom saddle was done, but there was no time. Perhaps after the battle.

Once Saga was happy with the way her gear fit, Jarl went in search of breakfast.

Brigid found him a few minutes later as he wandered toward the largest group of people and the scent of food.

"How are you feeling?"

"Better." Jarl stifled a yawn.

Brigid lifted her eyebrows. He shrugged.

"Good. Are you ready to play bait?"

"After I get some breakfast."

"This way."

"So what exactly do you want me to do?" He followed Brigid and accepted some oatmeal from a human cooking over one of the fires.

227

"We basically want you to go back to Vanaheim, be seen, and then get back here before they capture you." Brigid studied him.

He shook his head. "The risk of getting caught is pretty high." Jarl looked around and his gaze fell on Ima, where she stood with a couple of other Alfar discussing something.

"We do have a backup plan, but a lot hinges on you in this battle." Brigid glanced over at Ima then back at Jarl, tilting her head in question.

Jarl shook his head in reply, realizing he had been staring. "I don't know if Ima can cast the spell without me. I only say that because I'm fairly certain I couldn't do it very effectively without her. Is there another way?"

William came up behind them, looking much better than he had the other day. "The only other way we've thought of is to send one of us on basically a suicide mission where we tell your folks where you're hiding. They will likely imprison or kill us. All other feasible options take too long."

"And it really won't matter if the Vanier suspect a trap, because they'll feel they are safe behind their powers," Brigid continued.

"Very well. I'll go."

We will go, Saga said listening in.

No, I'll go. If something happens to me the others will need to know right away.

Jarl could feel Saga's frustration, but the Traveler knew he was right.

William patted Jarl on the shoulder and walked off. Jarl stared after him. Maybe saving the man's life had changed his views a little.

"When can you leave?"

"Whenever you are ready. If they're going to follow me, it won't take long," Jarl replied.

"Then go. I'll spread the word. We're basically ready." Brigid walked away.

Jarl went to where Saga grazed with Dance and Rainer. He put his arms around his friend's neck and leaned in, smelling her dry, dusty scent. She hugged him back.

Be careful. I will be ready for you when you return.

"I will." Jarl patted her shoulder and then gathered his Farer powers around himself and envisioned the courtyard around the palace he once called home.

He could tell the energies were different than the last time he had attempted to take himself there with his own power. He found a spot that seemed reasonably undisturbed and transported himself there. Using his power without the Crystal's assistance was getting easier, but going between worlds still wasn't as effortless as it once had been.

When he stepped out of the fog his power created into the courtyard, he gasped. A great deal of the keep still burned, and the palace that had been added on in ages past was nearly gone. The walls on this side of the stone building were rubble and the city beyond didn't look much better.

Clearly the Vanier hadn't been expecting such a direct attack, and it had been quite successful.

No one noticed him, though many people milled about in the courtyard. Some moved with purpose, others seemed lost. Jarl tried to feel bad, then he remembered the poisoned rain that had fallen on the Travelers' home world and all sympathy left him.

He grabbed the arm of the next person to rush past him. "Conor Weland, where is he?"

The man, a guard by the looks of his clothing and the Crystal emblazoned across the front of a boiled leather breastplate, gestured vaguely. "Probably in the stables. It's the only building not on fire."

Jarl headed to the stables while the guard hurried off on whatever errand he had been on. A bunch of people milled around in front of the stables, some of them wearing blue. Jarl hesitated, then saw Conor arguing with another mage.

Already preparing his escape and trying to ignore his racing heart, Jarl approached the group.

Unlike the guard, it didn't take long for the mages to recognize Jarl. They all stared for a moment in stunned silence.

"Jarl," Conor said. "You have quite the nerve coming here."

"Did you hear what my mother did to the Travelers' home?"

"Does it matter compared to this?" Conor growled.

"She destroyed the entire world and killed so many. This is nothing compared to that." Jarl hadn't meant to get into much of a conversation, but for some reason he felt it important that Conor knew what had happened.

The other mage was silent for a moment before he shook his head. "Well, why are you here then?"

"You will leave us alone. That's all we want."

Conor snorted. "Not much luck there. Your mother won't rest until she's destroyed you and enslaved the Travelers. Your father was killed in the attack."

Conor delivered the news with little emotion. Jarl couldn't even begin to have feelings about that news. It was like something distant, and not real.

"What did you do with Ceridwen?" Conor's eyes narrowed.

"She's safe. The Travelers are supposed to return her once the conflict is over. We didn't want her getting hurt." Jarl glanced around, but so far no one was casting magic in his direction.

"You don't understand, Jarl. We won't leave you alone. You won't get what you want." Conor clenched his hands and glared at Jarl.

Timbers crackled and part of the remaining keep crashed to the ground.

Jarl flinched, almost bolting as his heart skipped a beat. He couldn't leave until they would follow.

"Fine. Then we will continue to fight, but remember, all we want is to be left alone." That wasn't quite true, but Jarl knew this really wasn't a negotiation, it was bait and that's all it had to be.

Jarl saw it the moment Conor and the other mages drew on their magic through his magesight. He stepped backward and let his powers envelop him and transport him away. Hopefully they would follow quickly. Though he didn't want to fight the others, that was all that was left in this conflict.

Saga nickered as soon as he stepped onto the grassy meadow.

"Warn everyone, my friend. They're coming."

Saga sent out the message and he mounted when she stepped to his side.

Chapter 33

Though in reality it didn't take that long, it felt like a small eternity for Saga as she waited with Jarl. They stood next to Rainer and Ima, waiting for the attack.

Saga's and Rainer's ears perked forward moments before a fog appeared across the field from them. It cleared quickly, revealing a small army's worth of armed men and women. In the front stood Jarl's mother.

She had come out of the fog of the Farer power ready to cast a spell. Blue energy crackled around her. Saga sensed that Jarl threw up shields around him, Ima, and the Travelers. If she was going to cast another world-ending spell, everyone would simply have to flee.

Nessa thrust her hands out toward Jarl and yelled something as she released the spell.

It spread rapidly and dissipated into shining blue motes.

Saga shivered as they momentarily coated the shield Jarl held, but didn't penetrate.

"What did she do!" Ima gasped.

"I don't know," Jarl said, worry making his voice tight, "it was a big spell, she's going to need a minute to recover. Let's go."

Saga's skin tingled as Jarl and Ima joined their powers. He wove the spell to destroy the Crystal parasite.

He maintained the shield, but all they could do was focus on weaving the magic. It was up to Saga and Rainer to protect their partners.

The Vanier soldiers charged and a few of the other mages also cast spells at Jarl and Ima, though a few of the spells were targeted at the fake camp.

Ima and Jarl had worked together so much at this point, that Jarl was able to maintain the shield while he worked with the Alfar's help, and it was strong enough to deflect the spells, though Saga couldn't help but back away as magic flashed around them.

The foot soldiers closed in, and Saga gripped her sword, prepared to fight. As soon as the soldiers were committed to the charge, the archers hidden in the forest, rock outcroppings and up in the mountainside fired.

Humans screamed and fell, and the soldiers farther back skidded to a halt, confusion at the sudden attack sending them into disarray.

The Vanier outnumbered the Travelers and their human and Alfar partners, but the deadly arrows rained down from cover, evening the odds as soldiers dropped, screaming to the ground. Now if only Jarl could damage the mages.

"Now!" Jarl dropped the shield and cast the spell just as the first of the soldiers arrived.

Saga reared and struck out as soon as the spell left Jarl's hands. The man fell beneath her hooves.

Rainer charged forward and shouldered another man out of his way, biting at a third.

Ima and Jarl sagged with the effort of casting the spell, clutching mane and saddles to stay on board while their mounts whirled.

A moment later, Jarl clutched his head and gasped in pain as shouts from the mages in the Vanier army echoed his distress.

Are you okay? Saga asked as she kicked out at a human who got to close.

"Yes, I'm just getting an echo of what the other mages are feeling. Still tied to the Crystal a bit, I guess," he said through gritted teeth.

"We should fall back," Ima shouted as she drew her sword, main spell casting duties behind her.

"Yes," Jarl agreed.

The mages have been injured. Full attack, Saga signaled.

Saga! We can't talk to our partners! Dance replied.

Do your best. Saga didn't have time to worry about Dance's words. It must have had something to do with the spell Nessa cast. She spun and kicked. A woman swung her sword at Saga's face, and Saga twisted her neck, managing to block with her own sword.

The woman's eyes widened, and Saga leapt forward, hoping she didn't know the solider. The woman fell beneath Saga's hooves.

Both Travelers turned to run before they were completely surrounded.

Jarl straightened, recovering from the backlash from the parasite's destruction. Before the Travelers could completely disengage, arrows rained down from the Vanier archers.

Jarl threw up a shield. He was a moment too slow. Ima cried out and slumped forward in the saddle.

"Ima!" Jarl grabbed for her shoulder. Saga felt her life fading away as the Alfar slipped from the saddle.

Rainer screamed in rage as his second partner died.

Rainer, we have to go.

The gray Traveler charged into the battle.

Saga would never talk him out of his attack. She'd have done the same if Jarl had fallen.

"Ima!"

She's gone, Jarl.

He gasped, and Saga felt his rage overtake his better judgement as he pressed with his legs, asking her to return to the fight.

Saga turned at his request and used the path Rainer had created trying not to trip on bodies as she raced after the other Traveler. She dodged soldiers full of arrows, a few still screaming in pain. She ignored the smell of emptied bowels, and the occasional splatter of gore where Rainer had taken down a foe and trampled them in the process.

Jarl, not even trying to conserve his energy now, tossed spells at the enemy taking out swaths of soldiers. They scattered, fear in their eyes at his fury.

More Vainer fell to the archers hidden in the rocks and trees, but the Travelers' fighters were moving out to engage and the arrows fell less frequently.

Nessa, now standing with straight back, green magic flickering around her arms, a crazed look in her eyes, threw her hands out toward Rainer.

Jarl dropped his own shield and flung it around the enraged Traveler. The green crackle of energy surrounded Rainer for a moment before dissipating off Jarl's shield. Rainer continued chasing down soldiers and trampling them and Saga wasn't sure if he had noticed the momentary protection or not.

Jarl's sword was in his hand now, and he aided Saga as they attacked the guards around Nessa.

Saga glanced at Nessa and saw her eyes widen as she watched her son and Saga take out the guards. All

236

the years of training together made their movements coordinated. They didn't even need communication to know what the other would do; they could feel each other's movements until the last of the guards had fallen.

"Call off the attack and leave," Jarl said, panting from all the exertion.

"Die!" Nessa blasted them with a spell.

Her strength wasn't what it had been, but even without the Crystals enhancing her powers, she was strong, and Jarl's shield barely held at close range.

Saga fell back and Nessa followed.

Just keep up the shield, see if you can wear her out, Saga said.

If I can hold the shield. The strain in his voice worried her.

Saga continued to fall back as Nessa drove them toward the rocky cliffs.

Chapter 34

Sweat soaked Jarl's hair to his scalp and dripped into his eyes as he focused on maintaining his shields. He had to keep a bubble all the way around them because some of the spells would wrap around, and he still had to worry about attack from behind. Saga wasn't in a position to do much other than fall back either as his mother approached.

Even without the Crystal power, Nessa was a powerful mage with years more experience than Jarl had. It was all he could do to keep up the energy to deflect her spells, and he wasn't sure how much longer he could manage.

We need to distract her somehow, Jarl said.

Yes.

Before they could come up with some sort of plan, Conor appeared next to them. Possibly he had used magic to disguise himself, possibly Jarl had been so distracted that he just hadn't noticed the other mage approach.

"Shards," Jarl shouted as Conor blasted him with a spell and sent him flying sideways out of the saddle.

Saga screamed, and Jarl saw her strike Conor in the chest with both back feet, sending him flying in the other direction.

The attack cost Jarl his shield. He scrambled to his knees and tried to clear his head enough to recast it.

Nessa focused on Saga.

"Saga, run!"

The Traveler tried but there wasn't anywhere to go, with the rocky cliffs behind them, and Conor and Nessa boxing them in.

Jarl staggered to his feet and did the only thing he could think of, he charged his mother, tackling her to the ground just as she released her spell.

Saga whinnied, but he had disrupted her aim, and the spell shattered the rockface above them, sending boulders tumbling down around them.

I'm okay.

Jarl didn't look, busy with his mother.

She stared at him, eyes wide with madness. Even without the Crystals, blue light flickered in her eyes.

Jarl, behind you!

Jarl twisted in time to avoid a thrust from Conor's sword. Conor narrowly avoided killing Nessa and she turned her vacant gaze on him.

Conor flinched back.

Jarl scrambled to his feet. He had lost his sword somewhere. He still had his knife though and drew it.

Nessa got to her feet and chanted a spell Jarl knew but had never performed. It would stop his heart. It wasn't easy. Nessa obviously felt she had time. She might be right, with Conor there.

Jarl glanced at his former friend. Conor frowned, obviously aware of what Nessa intended. But they were both trying to kill him anyway, and a spell was just as good as a sword.

Saga screamed a challenge, and Conor turned just in time to get trampled.

Nessa's eyes widened, and Jarl darted forward, trying not to feel his knife scraping on a rib, or the hot rush of blood as he found her heart with his blade.

She didn't even cry out as the blue light faded from her eyes.

Jarl backed away as his mother's body crumpled to the ground.

Jarl! Saga called.

He turned, surprised to see Conor and Saga still engaged. He had survived her attack and held a broken shaft of wood in front of himself.

Jarl wiped the blood off his hand and formed a moderately less lethal, but quicker to prepare, spell than his mother had attempted to cast.

Saga reared.

Conor thrust with the spear.

He missed but the arrow that took Saga in the throat seemed to stop time for Jarl as he watched his friend collapse to the ground.

He had already lost everything else. He wasn't about to lose her, too. Jarl raced toward his friend.

"Jarl," Conor called.

Jarl growled at his former friend and released the spell.

Conor took the spell at point blank in the face. He gasped, and fell to the ground, clutching his throat.

Jarl wasn't sure if Conor would survive and he didn't care. He fell to his knees at Saga's side.

"Saga!"

Jarl, it's been a good adventure, Saga said.

"We're going to have plenty more. Hold still." He used the last of his reserves and gathered his magic.

"Jarl!"

He ignored the frantic shouts. It sounded like Brigid and William yelling at him. He had to save his friend.

The rock face, Jarl. You must go.

"Never without you."

Using magic, he dissolved the arrow. Blood sprayed out of the wound. He put his hands on her neck and cast a healing spell.

It won't be fast enough, Jarl. Go! Saga's voice faded but Jarl was determined.

Though his energy flagged, he needed to do this. Focusing fully on his friend, he cast another healing spell, one that would work for a long period of time. Then he cast a spell that would slow Saga until she was effectively in magical stasis until she healed.

The effort taxed him, and he sagged, energy gone.

"Jarl! The cliff is collapsing, get out of there!" William yelled.

Jarl twisted, seeing William and Brigid frantically gesturing for him to leave. He scrambled to his feet and stared up at the wall. It couldn't come down on his friend.

Too late, the cliff face gave way.

"Shards!" Jarl shouted. He threw the last of his strength into a shield spell over him and Saga as the rocks came crashing down on top of them. Jarl fell to his knees as the shield spell shrank as his energy flagged. The sound of falling rock drowned out everything else.

He had to do something. Though he hated to do it, he opened himself to the trickles of Crystal power he had felt from the growth on this world. It wasn't much, but he tied his shield to the Crystal's power and collapsed across his fallen friend's body, completely drained from the effort. He hoped the shield would hold long enough for him to rest. He would be able to dig them out after he had a little sleep.

His eyelids drooped and his last conscious thought was to remember a warning about the stasis spell. It would affect any living being touching it.

He cursed, tried to move off Saga. Unconsciousness took him before he could prevent the spell from dragging him to sleep.

Chapter 35

A surge of energy blasted through Jarl, and he snapped his eyes open. He stared at two human-like shapes. The bright blue sky above him shadowed their faces. One of the humans collapsed backward into the other's arms.

Saga!

Here!

"Who in Egil's name are you?" He scrambled to his feet. His body didn't want to cooperate, and he staggered, clutching his head with numb feeling hands.

"We're friends," the woman said.

He could make out their features a little better now. The woman had short, reddish hair and light colored but tan skin. She wore rough clothing that made him think of the Travelers. The man she held cradled in her arms had darker red hair and a faint hint of freckles across his pale skin.

They both collapsed backward and lay on the ground, as if exhausted after a long magical battle.

"We're friends," the woman said again. "Trying to wake you before the Vanir got you."

Her accent was strange, but understandable. He watched while she tried to free herself from underneath her unconscious friend. Jarl studied the man. He looked like he might be Vanir from his features.

"The Travelers are fighting them off. We need to leave."

"Not without the Travelers," Jarl said. If she thought he would leave Saga, especially after their last battle…

The woman stared at Jarl for a moment as if he were daft. "Of course not. How would we leave without them?"

Jarl frowned then glanced toward the Travelers battling humans in the distance. Clearly something deeper was going on. The woman knew who he was but didn't actually seem to know anything about him. Strange.

"Saga!"

His friend reared and struck at one of the combatants. The Travelers were able to disengage and race back toward him.

Saga whinnied, almost running him over in her haste to get to him. He took her sword and threw his arms around her. "My friend, I thought I'd never see you again."

Jarl, we are in the future!

What? "Later, we have to go! Amir, come here."

He came over and lay on the ground next to the humans.

Jarl helped when the woman tried to get her unconscious friend on the back of the gray Traveler. She got on behind him, and he briefly wondered who was partnered with who as the bay Traveler watched both anxiously.

Amir scrambled to his feet, Jarl helping to steady the man and woman. As soon as they were steady, he swung up onto Saga's back.

Magical energy prickled the hair on the back of Jarl's neck and he saw another unfamiliar woman about to blast all of them with a spell. What he did recognize was the slightly crazed look in her eyes.

The world blurred around them, colors running like wet paint as he heard someone shout: "Follow them!"

They shifted from world to world. Jarl clutched Saga's mane and tried not to think too hard about how exhausted he was.

Jarl, Saga said while they raced the *Through* ahead of any possible pursuit. *The other Travelers tell me that the spell your mother cast has caused a barrier between our kind. No one can directly speak anymore. The ones we Travel with are Sabaska and Amir. Anna rides Sabaska and Cahir is Amir's partner.*

She must have done it to keep the Travelers from easily coordinating battles.

Likely. It has been a couple of hundred years or more since the battle. So long that the Travelers we are with don't actually know many of the details, but still we fight. We must end things in this time.

I agree, Saga. Clearly this has gone on long enough.

Jarl felt sick that their battle hadn't ended the war. He still had his mother's blood on his hands, and Saga's blood soaked into his leather armor. He didn't know if Conor had survived, and it was likely everyone he had ever known, besides Saga, was long dead anyway.

What happened, why did we sleep so long?

I cast a stasis spell on you, so you could heal. I forgot it would put me into stasis too, if I was touching you.

It is a good thing you excel at shields.

247

A very good thing. Jarl didn't tell her he had used the Crystal magic to keep them alive. He wasn't sure if she would actually care or not, but he didn't want to think about it.

He had so many questions, but he doubted the people he currently traveled with had any answers.

They finally stopped on a dry, dusty grassland. Though drought had obviously been a problem for a while as the grasses were short.

The Travelers nibbled to recover their strength. Everyone was drenched in sweat, and Jarl sagged in the saddle.

Jarl noticed Anna studying him. "We will rest here for a short time and see if the Vanir catch up to us," he said. "If they don't, then we can go where Sabaska would lead us."

"Okay."

"Are you well?"

"Yeah. I think I'm fine. Cahir's badly injured though."

Saga dropped back so that she walked next to Amir, and Jarl studied the pair of humans.

"How long have we slept?" He studied Anna.

"Um, I'm not really sure. I gathered from the story I heard that it was a long time."

"Truly, I didn't intend for that. I was only trying to save Saga."

For which I am grateful, the Traveler replied.

"Wait, how come I can hear her when she's talking to you?"

"She's including you in on the conversation. I take it no one broke the magic my mother cast?" He knew the answer to that as well, but was curious about her response.

"If you're talking about the magic that prevents us from communicating with them, no, it's still there."

Jarl sighed. "That's too bad. I'll do my best to fix it once I've rested."

"You're handling this very well."

He smiled, though he barely had the energy to do it. She had no idea the turmoil that churned through his mind. In the end it didn't matter. He was here and so was Saga. "I'm too tired to worry very much about anything right now. Besides, Saga is with me." Jarl could see that Anna smiled, understanding softening her features.

We should continue, Saga said. *I don't like the way Cahir's breathing sounds.*

"I believe we are safe to Travel on. They would have caught up to us by now if they were going to."

"You're sure?"

"Yes, Sabaska, please lead the way."

The little bay Traveler tossed her head, and Saga followed her into the *Through.*

Chapter 36

The world that came into focus around them felt damp, a little chilly after the warmth of the dry plains they had rested on. Large trees, both in height and girth, lined the cart path the Travelers cantered down.

Cahir sagged badly in the saddle, and Jarl wondered if he should attempt to use his magic to heal him. He truly didn't feel up to the effort. He would try if necessary.

For as long as we slept, I feel like we should be better rested, Saga said.

I think it has more to do with our abrupt awakening after so long asleep.

"We're here, at least for now," Anna said.

The bay Traveler whinnied and increased her speed.

"She's going to let them know we're coming," Anna said.

"Very well," Jarl replied, wondering who *she* was.

Saga and Amir slowed to a walk, and Anna sighed, shoulders relaxing.

The silence stretched between them, and though it wasn't uncomfortable Jarl finally broke it. "I'm Jarl, by the way. It seems you've already been introduced to Saga."

They knew who we were.

"Hi, Jarl. I'm Anna. This is Cahir. He's the one who woke you and Saga. Amir is his partner."

"He's Vanir, isn't he?" Jarl studied the unconscious man.

"Yes," Anna answered.

"What made him join the Travelers?"

"I…" The woman hesitated. "I don't know. Me, I think."

Jarl had wondered if that was the case. "He's a lucky man then."

Anna blushed.

The trees thinned, and they broke into a clearing. A pair of buildings stood in the middle. One looked more like a brightly painted house and the other more barn shaped.

"We're here."

Amir broke into a canter, and after a quick moment to make sure Jarl was ready, Saga followed. The barn doors stood open and Amir went straight inside. He stopped by a human couch, and Jarl was amazed to see Traveler shaped bowl couches, too.

Jarl quickly dismounted and helped Anna get Cahir onto the couch

"Anna, you did it!" A darker-skinned woman with tightly curled black hair ran over to them. "Of course, I'm pissed you left me here."

She and Anna hugged, and then she offered to take care of the Travelers.

"Hello, Jarl," a very familiar musical voice said.

Jarl spun around, eyes wide.

"Linny?" He rushed over and crushed the Alfar in a hug. Saga was right behind them, wrapping both in the Traveler's version of a hug.

"Shards, Linny, I never thought I'd see you again, either." He couldn't even comprehend how glad he was to see a familiar face. Especially Orlinza. He had managed to come to terms with the idea that everyone

252

he knew was gone, but he hadn't taken into account the long-lived Alfar.

"I thought you were lost, as well. We have much to catch up on. Cahir is badly injured. I must tend to him first. Karen can show you the facilities and food is on its way."

Jarl hugged her one more time and then followed Karen in a bit of a daze. He went through the motions of caring for Saga and himself in something of a blur and then he went to find Orlinza.

Saga followed.

She met them out in the pasture where the other Travelers grazed, and then led them to her house.

"Orlinza, what happened?"

She sighed. "I don't truly know all the details, as I wasn't there. I will fill you in as best I can. Many were killed. As you were able to weaken the mages, the fight was reasonably even. Brigid and William survived, though Dance fell in the battle. She said he was so badly wounded that she had to help him cross to the next life. She...never took another partner."

Jarl's shoulders sagged and he clenched his fists. He was glad for the details, though everything was still fresh for him, as if it had just happened.

"I know most of what I can tell you from Brigid and William." Orlinza put her hand on Jarl's shoulder. "There's more. Your mother did not survive the battle. You know that?"

Jarl held out his hands. "I killed her."

Orlinza nodded. "No one was sure, but that is what we thought. Conor," she hesitated, "also fell."

Jarl sagged into a chair and stared at his hands. He had killed his best human friend and his mother.

"I know," he whispered.

Orlinza didn't press for details, for which Jarl was grateful. Saga nudged Jarl, and he put a hand on her shoulder.

"What happened to Ceridwen?" At least he knew she had been safe from battle.

"She chose to stay with the Alfar. Lady Ailis joined the Travelers in their fight against the Vanir."

"I hope she wasn't too mad at me."

"She wasn't mad, just annoyed at the time. She was devastated when we told her you had been lost in battle. She made a good life with the Alfar."

Jarl smiled through a sheen of tears he hadn't noticed until they tracked down his cheeks.

"The damage dealt to the Vanier, well, they haven't recovered completely. So many mages were killed in the prior attack and that battle. They lost quite a lot of their knowledge, for which we can all be grateful."

Jarl clenched his jaw, though he couldn't disagree.

"You are, perhaps, the only mage alive with any truly significant magical knowledge beyond how to use magic in battle. At least in the worlds the Travelers and the Vanier are concerned with."

"That's quite the burden."

"Yes. From what I understand, Vanaheim is still mostly a ruin, though they've rebuilt some. Mageheim was overrun with Ovttar and is abandoned. No one knows how to cast the magic to destroy the Crystal, so the only weapon we have is the dust. I must tell you how it is created. Enough of us know so that knowledge is not in danger of being lost. You must teach others the magic necessary to destroy the Crystal. Perhaps Cahir will learn. I believe Karen is eager, though I'm not sure if she has the talent. Anna, she does, but I sense that the ability makes her nervous for some reason."

"I will see what I can do."

"The most important thing you can do is release the Travelers from the spell that prevents them from true communication. It has hindered efforts to defeat the Vanier, as your mother intended."

"That will be my first task." Jarl smiled. "And then we'll see about ending the parasite once and for all. We have to find the source and we need to destroy it."

"You will need help," Orlinza said.

"Seems like we have a capable and willing group in the next building." Jarl glanced in the direction of the barn.

"Yes. There are complications. They can likely be dealt with."

Jarl grinned through his tears. "There are always complications."

And as long as we have each other, we will prevail, Saga added. *No matter how long it takes.*

Jarl hugged Saga and tried not to think about everyone he had lost in this war. Though there was resistance before he and Saga had gotten involved, it was truly a war he and Saga had started, and it had gone on far too long.

It is time to finish this.

Yes, my friend. Together, we will end this.

The End

Jarl and Saga's adventures continue at the end of Sabaska's Quest.

Other Works

Tales of the Travelers
–Sabaska's Tale
–Sabaska's Quest

Legends of the Travelers
–Saga
–Jarl
–Saga's War

Doc Vampire Hunting Dog
–The Moths of Miller Place
–Camping Tales
–Sheep Interrupted (These Vampires Still Don't Sparkle)

Into the West

Sky Yarns
–Serpent Queen

Clanless Series
–Senior Year Bites
–Summer Break Blues
–Freshman Year Freaks

Brown Ghost Hunting Dog Collection

Various Short Stories
–Darkness Taken – Dragonthology
–The Baron and the Firebird – Happily Ever Afterlife
–And other various stories appearing in anthologies

About the Author

J.A. Campbell

When Julie is not writing she's often out riding horses, or working sheep with her dogs. She lives in Colorado with her three cats, Kira and Bran, her border collies, her Traveler-in training, Triska, and her Irish Sailor. She is the author of many Vampire and Ghost-Hunting Dog stories the Tales of the Travelers series, and many other young adult books. She's a member of the Horror Writers Association and the Dog Writers of America Association and the editor for Story Emporium fiction magazine.